The Amorous Spotted Slug for State Slug

And other Short Stories

By Larry Buege

Gastropod Publishing
126 Ridgewood Dr.
Marquette, Michigan 49855

Books by Larry Buege

Bear Creek (Humorous)
Miracle In Cade County (Mystery/Love Story)
Cold Turkey (Political Satire)
Super Mensa (Techno-Thriller)
William Goodman: Civil War Horsesoldier
Growing Up In Sparta (Autobiography)
The Amorous Spotted Slug (Short Stories)

Native American Series:
Chogan and the Gray Wolf
Chogan and the White Feather
Chogan and the Sioux Warrior
Chogan and the Winnebago Merchant
Chogan and the Vision Quest

Published by Gastropod Publishing,
Marquette, Michigan
Copyright © 2025 by Larry Buege

Library of Congress Control Number: 2025901668
ISBN: 979-8-9872588-6-6

Preface

There was a time when short stories were king. They were published in newspapers, *Reader's Digest*, The *New Yorker*, and many other national magazines. Writers like O. Henry made decent livings solely from the short stories they wrote. Some stories such as *The Ransom of Red Chief*, *The Gift of the Magi*, and *The Secret Life of Walter Mitty* have become classics. I read them in high school English classes and am all the better for it.

Today few magazines and almost no newspapers print short stories. When they do print a story, they provide little more than bragging rights for the authors. Over the years I have written many short stories, but none were submitted for commercial use. I wrote them for the personal satisfaction of placing stories on paper. My short stories have received regional and international recognition, so I have accumulated some bragging rights for my endeavors. I am now sharing them with readers who do not have time in their busy lives to read an entire novel.

My stories are written in a variety of genres. I do enjoy a good laugh and probably too many of my stories are humorous. They are marked by asterisks (*) so readers looking for more serious literature can bypass them.

I am not a poet, but I did include one poem. I wrote *The Wall* as self-therapy while I was recovering from PTSD. At the time PTSD had yet to be defined. There was no treatment; however, I found writing therapeutic. I only know two people on the Vietnam Wall by name, but there are twenty or thirty individuals with whom I was a participant as they joined that sacred list. Sometimes it was little more than filling a body bag; other times it was a heroic effort that failed. They are now old memories and I have moved on, but there was one death that haunts me the most. *The Wall* is dedicated to my personal unknown soldier.

Contents

*The Amorous Spotted Slug
A Yooper Legend

Oral history conveyed through innumerable generations, suggests Amorous Spotted Slugs migrated to Michigan's Upper Peninsula from the depths of the Amazon Jungle. According to the local folklore, a primitive tribe of Amorous Spotted Slugs discovered a flyer nailed to the trunk of a jungle palm tree. "Free Ocean Cruise," the flyer boasted. "Animals of All Kinds Welcome." The ship would sail (rain or shine) in thirty days. A gentleman by the name of Noah was organizing the excursion.

By nature, Amorous Spotted Slugs are party animals. So the entire tribe signed up for the cruise and set off on the long trek to the port of departure. After a thirty-day forced march they had traveled forty-two inches. Then the heavens unleashed a great downpour, and water inundated the low lands and began to cover the earth.

"Help, what shall we do?" one of the slugs cried out.

"We are doomed," replied a unicorn splashing through a nearby puddle, "but you can save yourselves." The unicorn pushed a floating coconut toward the slugs with his horn, and the Amorous Spotted Slugs quickly scampered aboard.

It rained forty days and forty nights, and water covered the land. The Amorous Spotted Slugs crafted a sail from a lily pad, but there was nowhere for the *Coconut Clipper*, as they now called their vessel, to sail. During a particularly violent storm, lightning struck the *Coconut Clipper*, knocking its crew on their posteriors. Fortunately, that segment of the average Amorous Spotted Slug's anatomy is built low to the ground. When they regained consciousness, they began experiencing visions of the future. The electrical charge had altered their brain chemistry making them clairvoyant.

One such vision suggested the water would part once the days began to wane and the nights became longer. The *Coconut Clipper* would then come to rest in a paradise exceeding their wildest desires. Finally, the days did begin to wane and the nights did become longer, but none of the voyagers was awake to greet the summer solstice. The *Coconut Clipper* jolted to a rest on Presque Isle, (now part of modern-day Marquette, Michigan). The sudden stop awoke one of the Amorous Spotted Slugs. He looked out at the virgin timber and lush green underbrush—this had to be the paradise of their vision.

"Yoo-pee! Yoo-pee!" he yelled to awaken the others. The remaining Amorous Spotted Slugs awoke and looked at the awaiting paradise.

"Yoo-pee! Yoo-pee!" they echoed. The name of the new land stuck and the Amorous Spotted Slugs became the first Yoo-pers.

To commemorate their long voyage, Amorous Spotted Slugs now celebrate the summer solstice (or "Yoo-pee, Yoo-pee" day as they refer to it) with a Thanksgiving Feast of pasties and Mackinac Island fudge. For dessert they serve coconut cream pie in tribute to the Great Coconut that carried them to the Promised Land.

*Slug in the Headlight
An Excerpt from the novel, *Cold Turkey*

I was driving home on a misty August evening when I saw it. There in the wash of my headlights, oblivious to the rain, sat an Amorous Spotted Slug. Like all Yoopers, I had heard tales of Amorous Spotted Slugs, but logic and common sense had cast doubt upon their existence. I slammed on my brakes and forced my car into a skid, hoping this would generate sufficient time for the A.S.S. to scamper away from my approaching tires, but it held its ground with that classic "slug in the headlights" look. The A.S.S. was waving a small brown object as if to draw my attention and then it disappeared under my chassis before I could discern the nature of its petition.

After my vehicle skidded to a stop, I dashed back to where I had last seen the A.S.S., hoping that somehow it had eluded my tires. But all that remained of the Amorous Spotted Slug was a streak of slime next to a small brown parcel. Using tweezers from the glove box, I carefully retrieved the object. It appeared to be a small book—no, a journal. According to local legend A.S.S. are not only preternaturally wise but also clairvoyant, capable of foreseeing events far into the future. Was the Amorous Spotted Slug trying to warn me of some cataclysmic future event? The A.S.S. had given its life while proffering the wisdom of the journal's contents. It was imperative that I continue the Amorous Spotted Slug's mission and convey its knowledge to the world. I returned home and, with the aid of a microscope, painstakingly transcribed the contents of the Amorous Spotted Slug's journal. These are its stories.

*The Purloined Pasty

Over the weekend Marquette city police received a two-eleven (robbery in progress) from an irate caller on the northwest corner of the Presque Isle. Central Dispatch sent officers Koski and Beaudry to investigate. They discovered Wally Higgenbottom sitting in his deer blind near Sunset Point, his hunting rifle leaning forlornly against the wall of the deer blind. Wally's wife arrived moments later. (She had been listening to the police scanner.)

"I think hunting season ended three weeks ago," Officer Koski suggested. Wally shrugged his shoulders.

"I told him so," his wife replied. "He never listens to me."

Since Wally was not actively hunting when the officers arrived, no citation was issued. That would have generated more paperwork than Koski was willing to tolerate this close to the end of his shift.

"Central Dispatch said you were being robbed." Officer Koski surveyed the spacious deer blind. A six-pack, bag of chips, and a dog-eared copy of an old Playboy Magazine rested on a wooden bench. "I don't see anything missing."

"My pasty's missing. The swine stole my pasty. I had it lying here on my bench. I turned my head for a moment and it was gone. I saw the thief drag it out the door."

"Can you describe the perpetrator?" Officer Koski took out his pad to take notes.

"The slimy thief was short—very short. And he had yellow skin."

"Chinese?"

"No, his skin was canary-yellow and covered with red, heart-shaped spots. He had two knobby antennas protruding from his head."

"He's been drinking again," Wally's wife surmised.

"Anything else? Did he say anything?"

"He did blow me a kiss just before he scampered away with my pasty."

A breathalyzer test revealed Wally was on the pleasant side of happy, but not legally drunk. Officer Koski closed his note pad; he had better things to do.

"Looky, looky," Officer Beaudry pointed to a trail of slime leading out the door.

"That's his trail," Wally said. "I told you he was slimy."

Officers Koski and Beaudry followed the trail through the door of the deer blind but quickly lost it in the underbrush.

"We need help," Officer Koski declared. He made a call on his cell phone and twenty minutes later another officer arrived with "Kasper the K-9 Kop" in tow. The dog handler pushed Kasper's nose into the slime and then turned him loose. Kasper loped off with a howl and disappeared into the woods. When the officers caught up to him, Kasper was vigilantly standing guard over a semi-circle of bakery crust—all that remained of a once-proud pasty.

"It was a decent pasty," Wally proclaimed.

"I'm sure the end came quickly," Officer Koski said.

"The pasty felt no pain," Officer Beaudry suggested.

While the officers were consoling Wally, Kasper ate the remaining evidence.

"You do know Wally's been drinking again," his wife said.

"You'll have to come back to the station and fill out a report," Officer Beaudry said, ignoring the wife's comment.

At the station a police sketch artist drew a picture of the perpetrator from Wally's description. The sketch was compared with a list of known Marquette County felons, but none had canary-yellow skin, with red heart-shaped spots and knobby antennas on his head. Working on a hunch, Officer Koski e-mailed the sketch to Professor Toivo Rantamaki. Rantamaki was the former chair of Paranormal Gastropod Psychology at Finlandia University and was currently in the depths of the Amazon Jungle researching his hypothesis that Amorous Spotted Slugs migrated from the Amazon Jungle to the U.P. on a coconut during the Biblical Flood. Professor Rantamaki sent a timely reply confirming that the perpetrator was, indeed, an Amorous Spotted Slug!

"Amorous Spotted Slugs have a weakness for pasties and Mackinac Island fudge," Rantamaki added. "Four husky Amorous Spotted Slugs can easily carry off a pasty." Reaction to the Professor's revelation was immediate and prolific. Authorities not only had a description of the thief, they now had a motive.

"We will apprehend this ruthless thief and bring him to justice," proclaimed the Police Chief. "Larceny of this magnitude will not be tolerated in Marquette. Not on my shift."

"Wally's been drinking again," Wally's wife suggested.

"We cannot judge all Amorous Spotted Slugs by the delinquent behavior of one miscreant A.S.S.," said a spokesperson for Travel Marquette. "We are hoping to make Marquette County the Amorous Spotted Slug capital of the U.P. It'll generate millions of tourist dollars."

Slug Lovers In Michigan Empowered released the following statement: Those of us at S.L.I.M.E. Headquarters extend our heart-filled sympathy for Mr. Higgenbottom's tragic and senseless loss. Although Amorous Spotted Slugs will occasionally borrow a pasty or perhaps some Mackinac fudge, they are lovable and harmless creatures and represent the preeminent virtues of the U.P., which is why we hope to make the Amorous Spotted Slug the official State Slug. The Lower Peninsula has the official State Stone (Petoskey Stone) and the official State Soil (Kalkaska Sand). It is only fitting that the U.P. have the official State Slug. To further our cause we are asking U.P. residents to report all A.S.S. sightings to our website (www.AmorousSpottedSlug.com).

The Marquette Mining Journal tried to contact Wally Higgenbottom for comment, but he was busy—he was at an AA meeting.

*Party Animals

Over the weekend Marquette city police received a breaking-and-entering complaint from a prominent Marquette resident. Central Dispatch sent Officers Koski and Beaudry with appropriate back-up to investigate. Finding nothing amiss upon arrival at the house in question, Officer Koski punched the doorbell. Wally Higgenbottom opened the door moments later.

"You called 911?" Officer Beaudry asked?

"They won't leave," Wally replied.

"Who won't leave?" Officer Koski asked.

"Amorous Spotted Slugs. The attic is infested with them."

"Who's at the door?" Ethyl Higgenbottom pulled aside the drapes on the front window. Members of Marquette's elite S.W.A.T. Team consisting of the police chief's hunting buddies were hunkering down behind trees and squatting behind parked squad cars. Weaponry varied from hunting bows to muzzle loaders, although deer rifles with high-powered scopes predominated. All weapons were pointing menacingly toward Ethyl's front door.

"Wally, there's a S.W.A.T. Team out there. You told me you paid your library fine!" Wally skillfully ignored his wife's accusation.

"Why are you guys dressed like that?" Ethyl asked when she joined Wally at the door. Large curlers cluttered Ethyl's hair leading Officer Koski to wonder whose appearance was more inappropriate.

"Someone called 911 and said you had intruders infected with Ebola."

Everyone looked at Wally. Wally shrugged his shoulders. "Didn't think you guys would come otherwise."

"Got any idea how difficult it is to maneuver a squad car in hazmat gear?" Officers Koski and Beaudry removed their hoods and goggles. They did not look happy.

Wally stared at the floor. "Does that mean you won't evict the intruders?"

"What makes you think they're Amorous Spotted Slugs?" Officer Beaudry asked.

"That A.S.S. who stole my pasty last year followed me home—must have liked my pasty. Now he's invited all his friends. They hold wild hoedowns every weekend."

"They're so cute," Ethyl offered.

"Can't get any sleep," Wally countered. "Their dance music is too loud."

"And you say they're in the attic?" Officer Beaudry examined the stairs leading to the attic and considered calling in back up. He could handle one A.S.S. but if the attic was truly infested with Amorous Spotted Slugs, he would need the S.W.A.T. Team.

Beaudry drew his nine millimeter and cautiously headed up the stairs, followed by Koski with a can of Pepper Spray in hand. When Beaudry reached the top of the stairs, he gingerly pushed open the trap door and climbed into the attic. Beaudry's posse consisting of Officer Koski armed with Pepper Spray and Ethyl armed with hair curlers followed closely behind him. Feeling prudence more appropriate than valor, Wally brought up the rear.

Beaudry scanned the attic with his Maglite. Except for a pile of boxes and some old lamps in the far corner, the attic was empty. "No evidence of Amorous Spotted Slugs," Beaudry proclaimed with some relief. Even the friendliest animals can become vicious when cornered. He had no desire to confront an A.S.S. in a dark attic no matter how amorous their reputation.

"They're hiding," Ethyl said. "They knew you were coming."

"They knew we were coming?" Officer Beaudry waited for an explanation.

"Ethyl thinks the A.S.S. are clairvoyant and can predict the future," Wally explained. "She spends too much time on the Internet."

"According to S.L.I.M.E.'s web site at AmorousSpottedSlug.com, Amorous Spotted Slugs became clairvoyant when lightning struck the coconut they were sailing on," Ethyl replied.

"Slime?" Koski wasn't sure he wanted to hear more. Central dispatch should have dispatched a psych team—with large nets!

"It stands for *Slug Lovers In Michigan Empowered.* S.L.I.M.E. nominated the Amorous Spotted Slug for State Slug. They're so cute."

"They steal pasties," Wally countered.

"Well, I don't see any slugs spotted or otherwise." Officer Beaudry again scanned the attic with his flashlight. The light came to rest on a square piece of wood the size of a cutting board. "What is that?" Beaudry asked.

"That's Ethyl's cutting board. They use it for a dance floor." Feeling it was now safe, Wally rejoined the others in the attic.

"They are such graceful dancers," Ethyl offered. "The choreography of their dance routines is delightful."

"Perhaps they're hiding under the cutting board," Wally suggested.

Officer Beaudry gave Wally's suggestion some thought. "Koski, I'll cover you while you flip over the cutting board." Beaudry leveled his pistol at the cutting board with his right hand while his quivering left hand maintained a beam of light on the board.

Koski considered voicing a complaint; he had a wife and child to consider. But he did not wish to display fear in front of civilians. He had his pride. "Here, hold my pepper spray, but don't press the top or it'll release the gas." Koski passed the canister to Wally and then cautiously approached the cutting board. Grasping the cutting board with trembling hands, he gingerly raised the board. Slimy yellow creatures scampered in all directions.

"Whoa!" Beaudry reflexively stepped backward into a pool of slime as a hoard of Amorous Spotted Slugs stampeded toward him. His hand impulsively tightened around his pistol as he fell, and a healthy dose of smokeless gunpowder propelled a nine-millimeter projectile into the cutting board Koski was holding. Wooden splinters were sent flying through the air.

"Don't let them get me!" Beaudry pleaded as he hit the ground.

"I got you covered!" Wally extended the pepper spray canister toward the approaching Amorous Spotted Slugs and pressed the top. Unfortunately, the nozzle was pointing toward Beaudry.

Wally's arraignment is scheduled for July 2nd.

*Amorous Spotted Slug for State Slug

It had been a long time since the old neighborhood had seen such excitement. The vacant lot, which had been home to the We Energy power plant on the north side of Marquette, was now crawling with every form of humanity. An insufficient assortment of police officers was gallantly trying to bring order to the chaos, but they were quick to admit their shortcomings. Flashing lights beamed from their squad cars in a vain attempt to magnify their presence.

In the center of activity, three bulldozers, engines in idle, sat helplessly while their operators and other construction workers conversed in small groups. Their frustration was palpable. Over a hundred highly vociferous protesters waving large posters and chanting a farrago of provocative pabulum surrounded the helpless construction workers.

Although unnecessary, a provocateur with a megaphone egged on the demonstrators.

Ethyl Higgenbottom, standing at the edge of the protesters, surveyed the chaos with pride. They had stopped them, at least for the moment. It would be sufficient to obtain a court order, and that was what mattered. There would be no further development here. With environmental impact studies and frivolous lawsuits, she could keep them tied up for years.

It didn't take long for the media to arrive (they had been alerted in advance). Helicopters armed with telephoto lenses circled above as camera crews set up satellite dishes to provide live feed to the eagerly waiting world. They would be just in time for the six o'clock news. A TV newscaster thrust a microphone into Ethyl's face.

"Mrs. Higgenbottom, I'm Rob Carter from the Channel 6 News in Negaunee. Can you tell us what this protest is about?"

Ethyl smiled at the man with the camera on his shoulders. Form is everything, she told herself. "I'm glad you asked, Rob. We are concerned citizens who are fighting to save the Amorous Spotted Slug."

"Did you say spotted slug?"

"Yes, Rob. But this is not just any slug. The Amorous Spotted Slug is currently on the endangered species list and is normally found only in Marquette's Presque Isle Park. Many felt they could not thrive anywhere else."

"Are you saying they are now propagating on the grounds of this old power plant?"

"That's correct, Rob. Two days ago several of these extremely rare slugs were found right here in the remnants of this old coal pile. That's why it is so important we leave the land in its pristine beauty."

The newscaster looked around at the scattered lumps of coal, old tires, and other trash. Only in minds of the visually impaired could such a pigsty be considered pristine beauty. "Amorous Spotted Slug, that's a strange name for a slug. What makes it so important?"

"Rob, most people are unaware of this wonderful creature's natural beauty. I recently talked with Toivo Rantamaki, Professor Emeritus of Finlandia University, on the phone who describes the sex life of the Amorous Spotted Slug as unique within the animal kingdom. Professor Rantamaki says before the Amorous Spotted Slugs copulate they perform this ritualistic mating dance, which is quite intricate. Each subspecies has a slightly different cadence. Professor Rantamaki says the choreography is unbelievable."

"Have you seen this mating dance?"

"No, Rob, I haven't. Unfortunately, the A.S.S. is nocturnal and is seen best with night-vision goggles. The A.S.S. tend to be very slow, which is why they're so rare. The mating dance can take hours, and often one of the A.S.S. will fall asleep before they copulate. The mating dance is quite meaningful when seen in time-lapse photography."

"And these slugs are normally found only at Presque Isle Park? That's just a ways down the road."

"That's right, Rob. Professor Rantamaki believes they originated in the Amazon Jungle and migrated to Michigan's Upper Peninsula on drifting coconuts during the Great Biblical Flood. As you know, the unicorns were less fortunate. Professor Rantamaki says the A.S.S. can't propagate below the bridge, because Trolls carry a virus that is often lethal to the A.S.S. We hope to make the Amorous Spotted Slug the official state slug. The Petoskey Stone is our official state stone and the Kalkaska Soil is our official state soil, but we have nothing unique to the U.P. The A.S.S. would make the perfect state slug."

"Mrs. Higgenbottom, are you aware there are plans to build a school for blind paraplegics on the site of the old power plant?"

"Rob, sometimes we have to make sacrifices for the good of this planet we live on. I'm sure, when all of those blind paraplegic kids see what we've done, they'll leap with joy."

"How did you happen to find these slugs?"

"That's rather weird, Rob. Someone phoned in an anonymous tip, which is strange since few people would recognize an Amorous Spotted Slug."

"I see not everyone is enthralled with the A.S.S. You have some counter protesters."

"Rob, I believe that would be protester, in the singular. Wally gets some strange ideas, especially when he's been drinking."

"Let me get his take on the Amorous Spotted Slug."

The TV 6 reporter worked his way through the crowd toward a lone protester holding up a *Deport the A.S.S.* sign.

"Excuse me, sir. I'm Rob from the TV 6 News. Are you Wally? Can you tell me why you're protesting against this loveable slug?"

"They stole my pasty."

"They stole your pasty?"

"Yep. Two years ago I was hunting deer on Presque Isle, and one of those &#%# slugs stole my pasty. Then last year they infested my attic—wild parties every night—couldn't get any sleep. They're a public nuisance. Now Ethyl wants to make them the state slug. Those Amorous Spotted Slugs are an invasive species, illegal aliens. They should be deported back to the Amazon Jungle."

"How do you feel about making the Amorous Spotted Slug the official state slug?"

"Over my dead body! Ethyl spends way too much time on Facebook with those environmental groups. Those lascivious slugs are destroying our marriage. Half the time, Ethyl doesn't even have time to fix dinner."

"You're married to the protest leader?"

"Yeah, but don't print that. It could ruin my credibility."

***

Officers Koski and Beaudry were patrolling the donut shops in north Marquette when they received the call: "Hostile protesters blocking traffic at the Presque Isle Park entrance. Officers on the scene requesting backup." It was not a welcomed assignment this close to the end of their shift, but Koski and Beaudry were the only officers on duty with riot training. Koski took a bite from his nut-covered donut and brushed the crumbs from his uniform. With everybody armed with cell-phone cameras, it never hurt to look his best.

"Hit the siren and lights," Beaudry suggested. A flashy arrival with a modicum of police brutality often defused tense conflicts, at least that was the lie Beaudry told himself.

"It must be that women's lib group again," Koski said, referring to a small group of women advocating the removal of Father Marquette's statue. It was a flagrant sexist symbol of male domination, at least from their viewpoint. Why Father Marquette and not Mother Marquette? They normally protested early in the day to ensure coverage by the evening news.

Koski turned the police cruiser onto Lake Shore Drive and headed toward Presque Isle. Residents called it an island, but in reality it was a small peninsula jutting into Lake Superior. All the land and adjacent marina were part of the city park system. It was a popular spot for boaters, bikers, and star gazers. Presque Isle came into view as they crossed the Dead River Bridge.

"Holy Wah!" Koski dropped his donut mid bite. "There must be several hundred people in that mob."

"Should we request additional backup?" Beaudry asked as his trembling hands reached for the mike. "Maybe National Guard?"

"Let's check it out first," Koski replied. "They seem peaceful." He had a new can of pepper spray he was itching to try out. Koski was several years senior to Beaudry and activating the National Guard would show signs of weakness.

Koski stepped out of the car and stretched out his five feet, six inch frame. A CNN helicopter was hovering overhead. Down below hundreds of energetic protesters were waving protest signs that stated, "A.S.S for State Slug." Koski assumed they were referring to the Amorous Spotted Slug. Koski had encountered them several times in the past— never with a good outcome.

Several officers were trying to usher the protesters away from the road. They would have had better luck transporting a load of frogs in a wheelbarrow. A long line of cars filled with irate occupants hoping to spend the day at Presque Isle waited impatiently for the protesters to clear a path. That was not about to happen.

"We need to find the ring leader," Koski said.

The leader was not hard to find. Ethyl was waving her "A.S.S. For State Slug" sign and working up the crowd with her megaphone. Wally was equally energetic as he waved his "Deport the A.S.S." Koski and Beaudry had encountered the couple several times in the past. They changed any minor disturbance into a disaster. The two officers weaved their way toward the center of the crowd.

"Officers Koski and Beaudry, it is so nice of you to join our protest," Ethyl said when she saw the officers approaching.

"We're not here to join your protest. You're blocking traffic. Unless you have a parade permit, you have to disperse."

"Are you going to deport those A.S.S.," Wally asked. "They're illegal aliens, ya know."

"Can I borrow your megaphone for minute," Koski asked. Assuming Koski was indeed joining her cause, Ethel passed over the megaphone.

"Listen up, everyone. The pasty shop on Presque Isle Avenue is giving away free pasties to the first one hundred customers."

"Is that true?" Beaudry asked. He was thinking a pasty would go well with the donuts.

"Heck if I know," Koski replied, but within five minutes, only officers Koski and Beaudry remained next to the lingering lumps of coal from the old power plant.

The Song of Minnehaha

"Sean, I went to town for groceries. I'll be back by noon. There's a breakfast burrito in the freezer. Nuke it for two minutes. And don't forget your insulin, ten units of regular and twenty of Lente."

Never marry a nurse; they always treat you like a patient. I've been taking insulin for twenty years. One would think that would suggest a modicum of medical knowledge. Despite her occasional nagging, Clara has been a good wife. I write "I'll be in the woods when you return" at the bottom of Clara's note and leave it on the kitchen table. My penmanship has never been great; now, with the tremors in my hands, it is barely legible.

I walk over to the fridge and remove the vial of regular insulin; I won't need the Lente today. The breakfast burrito also does not fit my plans. I place the insulin in a plastic grocery bag and head for the den.

We've been spending summers in this cabin overlooking Lake Superior for thirty years. It is no longer a second home; for me, it is home. This is where I found motivation to write. Some of my best works owe their conception to a small spark of inspiration gleaned from these forty acres of Upper Peninsula wilderness.

Most of the cabin belongs to Clara, but the den is mine. It is small, to be sure, but it provides my basic needs. The fabric on my red sofa is worn and frayed. If Clara had her way, it would have been banished to sofa heaven years ago. (It has too many memories for me to discard.) Up against the window overlooking Lake Superior is my oak desk. This is where I did my writing, first on a manual typewriter and then by computer. I say that in past tense since my tremors prevents all but the most essential writing. Now, only my dictionary and thesaurus remain on the desk. They were my workhorses, receiving extensive use as I searched for that elusive stronger verb or that more descriptive noun. Samuel Clemens purportedly said, "The difference between the right word and the almost right word is the difference between lightning and a lightning bug." Sam was a wise man.

The walls are covered with knotty pine, although bookshelves and pictures obscure much of it. Most of the pictures I took myself: local landscapes and spring flowers. One picture is of a much younger me accepting a Pulitzer Prize for my fifth novel. I find that a bit vain, but Clara insists it remains on the wall.

The bookshelves are where I store my memories and contain the more important books I have read over the years. Even now, as I look at the titles and then close my eyes, I can replay the stories in vivid detail. My memory is one of the few physical attributes that has not exsanguinated with age. My other senses have been relegated to the endangered species list. Despite three laser surgeries, doctors predict diabetes will claim my eyesight within a year.

Twenty-three books on the shelf have my name on the spine. I hope that is a worthy legacy of my life. It is a silly thing for an old man to think about. I pull an old, leather-bound book from the top shelf and add it to the insulin in my plastic bag. Of all the books on the shelf, this is the book I hold in highest esteem—even above those I have authored. I close the door to the den behind me and exit the cabin through the back door.

It will be a warm day. The matutinal sun is already above the trees, suffusing the clearing in which the cabin stands with sunlight. The radiant warmth feels good on my skin. I head down a well-worn path into the woods, a trip I make daily in the summer. The path is lined on both sides by trilliums, a sure sign of spring. It is one of nature's eternal truths; trilliums will be blooming in spring thousands of years after maggots have finished dining on my soul. About one hundred yards into the woods, the path opens into a clearing of sorts. The trees still provide a canopy overhead, but the ground has been cleared of underbrush, revealing a small brook. It is too small to qualify as a stream or even a creek. It is only two feet across at its widest spot and in the dry summer months is almost non-existent. The brook drains down from the hill above the cabin and culminates in a gentle waterfall of no more than three feet in height. The water gurgles as it cascades from one rock to the next.

I sit down on a reclining lawn chair I keep there for that purpose; even the short walk from the cabin leaves me tired. I write in my den, but this is where I think. The formula for a good novel, I have discovered, is two parts thinking and one part writing. I take the insulin from the bag and draw up 100 units; I assume that will be sufficient. Then I inject it into the subcutaneous tissue of my belly. I do not bother with the perfunctory alcohol swab.

I take the book out of the bag and caress the aged leather binding. Books have been my life, my sole reason for existence. That had not always been the case. I close my eyes and remember that summer day in 1954. The war in Korean had ended and times were good. I remember standing before that square edifice of red brick and stone that squatted on a small knoll overlooking Union Street on the north side of town in Sparta, Michigan. Its windows were tall and slender and arched at the top like a cathedral. Their lower ledges were well over six feet tall, precluding any thought of peering in—not that I cared to—and the door to the building was recessed in a cave-like structure covered by a high, vaulted arch of cut stone. A drawbridge would not have been out of place. The single word "Library" was etched in stone above the arched entrance.

I had walked past the building on my way to school, but I had never been inside. I had walked past many buildings on my way to school, none as formidable as that stone fortress now peering down on me. No other building so totally dominated the landscape or so filled me with trepidation.

Photo curtesy of Sparta Township Library

School was out for the summer, and fifth grade wouldn't begin until fall; I could find no logical reason for my being there. Summers were for fun and excitement. I should be standing on the pitcher's mound throwing fastballs in Little League and bowing to cheering crowds. Someday I would stand on the pitcher's mound at Tiger Stadium. When I closed my eyes I could hear the roar of the crowd as my fastball whipped over the plate for strike three. This was not to be; a cast on my right wrist prohibited any fastballs. I was out for the season.

With the summer in ruins and nothing significant to occupy my time, I had been relegated to errand boy, returning a library book for my mother. It was a degrading chore at best: books were for girls; baseball was for boys. My mother asked that I personally give the book to Mrs. Weaver, one of the librarians and a close friend of my mother. According to my mother, Mrs. Weaver was a full-blooded Ojibway. Weaver didn't sound very Indian to me.

Once I was assured none of my friends was watching, I slipped into the library. The inside was smaller than I had imagined. It was one large room with rows of bookshelves lined up like fields of corn. They were so tall I would have been unable to reach the top shelf, if for some unforeseen circumstance the need should arise. In the center, sitting at a large oak desk, guarding the books, was an elderly lady with hair that was not gray, but white like freshly fallen snow, and it billowed up in a bun like a snowdrift. Her skin was unusually tanned for this early in the summer. Hanging around her neck by a chain were a pair of turtle-shell glasses, a fitting accouterment to her profession. The name plaque on her desk identified her as Minne Weaver.

"Mrs. Weaver?" I said as I cautiously approached the desk as one would a trial judge.

She looked up and scrutinized all four-foot-two of me, paying particular attention to the flaming red hair protruding from under my Detroit Tigers baseball cap. "You must be Sean Connolly. I talked to your mother yesterday."

We had not previously met, but with my red hair, I was not difficult to pick out of a crowd. As the summer progressed, my face would be covered with freckles. The red hair I could tolerate; the freckles I could do without.

"Are you really an Indian?" I asked. "You don't look like an Indian." My mother would have been horrified by my question, but it was something any ten-year-old would need to know.

"You don't look much like Daniel Boone either," she replied. "You're thinking of historical Indians like you see in the movies." She opened her purse and pulled out a well-worn picture. "This is my grandfather."

I looked at the man in the black and white photo. He had dark skin and high cheekbones, and his hair was black with braids on both sides. Although he was wearing an old-style, tailored suit, he was very much an Indian. I could visualize him riding scout for John Wayne.

"There are many Indians in the Upper Peninsula where I grew up," she said. "My husband and I married after college. John worked for the mines as a geologist. When he died four years ago, I moved down here to work in the library."

Her eyes began to water—old people tend to get sentimental at times. I felt bad; I had only wanted to know if she was Indian. She grabbed a tissue from her desk and dabbed her eyes dry as if no explanation were needed.

"My mother asked me to return this book." I laid the book on her desk hoping the distraction would alleviate her sorrow.

She checked the due-date and set the book on a rolling cart half filled with books. Then she gave my red hair and cap another once over. "You must be a Tigers fan."

"Yes, ma'am. I'm going to play for the Detroit Tigers when I grow up. My uncle promised to take me to one of their games when he comes home from Korea." I looked down self-consciously at the cast on my wrist. "I fell off my friend's horse a couple of weeks ago and broke my wrist. I'd be playing ball now if it weren't for this." I held up my cast as exhibit "A."

"That can happen to any ballplayer. Even Casey had his bad days."

"Casey? Who'd he play for?" I had baseball cards for Babe Ruth, Ty Cobb, Mickey Mantle, and all the baseball greats, but I couldn't remember anyone named Casey. He had to be a minor leaguer.

"You never heard of Mighty Casey of the Mudville Nine?"

I felt a bit of shame. "No, ma'am."

"We need to correct that. I'll be right back." The lady disappeared into the cornfields and reappeared with a well-worn book. "Take this home and read "Casey at the Bat" on page twenty-nine." She handed me the book. The title of the book was *The Best of American Poetry*. I felt trapped. The noose was tightening around my neck and the trap door quivered beneath my feet. I couldn't just give the book back to her.

"Just make sure you return it in two weeks."

I left the library with the book of poetry under my shirt. If any of my friends were to see it, I'd never survive the razzing...and poetry of all books. Ten years old and my manhood was already in question. I gave the baseball field a wide berth to avoid any encounters with close friends and arrived home with my pride intact. I yelled a quick "hello" to my mother who was fixing dinner in the kitchen and headed upstairs to my room. I didn't feel safe until my bedroom door was securely closed behind me. I would hide the book under my mattress and smuggle it back into the library the following morning. No one would be the wiser.

Before Mighty Casey was sequestered in the safety of my mattress, I had to see who he was. I turned to page 29, finding "Casey At The Bat" by Ernest Lawrence Thayer.

The outlook wasn't brilliant for the Mudville nine that day.

The score stood four to two, with but one inning more to play,

And then when Cooney died at first, and Barrows did the same,

A pall-like silence fell upon the patrons of the game.

The legendary Harry Caray couldn't have better described the game. I continued reading down the page, fascinated with the rhythm of the story. It was as if I were there or at least listening to the play-by-play description on the radio. I had no doubt Mighty Casey would save the day.

Oh, somewhere in this favored land the sun is shining bright,

The band is playing somewhere, and somewhere hearts are light,

And somewhere men are laughing, and little children shout;

But there is no joy in Mudville? Mighty Casey has struck out.

The ending was a let down; I had wanted Casey to clear the bases. This was unlike any poetry I had ever read. There was no flowery language or mushy romance. It was a poem a boy could read without shame, not that I planned to tell anyone. I scanned the table of contents but found no more baseball poems. "The Midnight Ride of Paul Revere" piqued my interest; I liked horses. I turned to page 89.

Listen my children and you shall hear
Of the midnight ride of Paul Revere,

For the next few minutes I rode "through every Middlesex village and farm, for the country folk to be up and to arm." I could feel the wind in my face as my trusty steed galloped through the countryside. The horse's mane stung as it whipped across my cheek, but I didn't care. I rode through Lexington and on to Concord, all the time yelling, "The British are coming! The British are coming!" Finding nothing more of interest in the book, I stashed it under my mattress.

I returned to the library the following morning, my book safely tucked under my shirt. Mrs. Weaver was sitting at her desk overlooking her domain. I assumed defending her desk against all comers was part of her job description.

"Good morning, Mrs. Weaver. I'm returning your book."

"What did you think of 'Casey at the Bat'?"

"It was O.K., I guess. Is he a real person?"

"He can be if you want him to. Did you read any other poems?"

I wondered if conversations with librarians were privileged like talking to a priest or an attorney. "I read about Paul Revere."

"Ah, Longfellow, one of my favorite poets. Let me show you something."

She reached into one of her desk drawers and pulled out a brown paper bag. Inside was a book aged by time. It was bound in brown leather and trimmed in gold leaf. For a moment I feared she was going to pawn another book on me.

"This is one of the earliest editions of Longfellow's *Song of Hiawatha*. I'm told it's worth a lot of money— not that I would ever sell it. It tells about the adventures of a young Indian boy about your age named Hiawatha. Longfellow personally gave it to my grandfather." She opened it to the first page. "See." I looked at the page and saw Henry Wadsworth Longfellow scribbled in the margin. "My grandfather gave it to my mother, and she gave it to me. I had hoped to pass it on to my son or daughter, but John and I never had any children." Her eyes began to water again. She seemed to get teary-eyed every time she talked about her husband.

She opened the book to one of the earlier pages. "Listen to this: By the shores of Gitche Gumee by the shining Big-Sea-Water stood the wigwam of Nokomis."

"What's gitche gumee?"

"That's the Indian name for Lake Superior, where I grew up. Longfellow uses a lot of Indian names." She closed the book and carefully returned it to her paper bag. "Most people call me Minne, but my real name is Minnehaha. My mother named me after Hiawatha's lover. Minnehaha means waterfall in Dakota."

"Does the book have any horses in it?"

"I don't believe so. You like horses?"

"Yes, ma'am. I have a friend who lives on a horse farm. We ride them sometimes. That's how I broke my wrist. The horse got spooked and I fell off. It wasn't his fault."

"You fell off a horse and broke your wrist and you still like horses?"

"Yes, ma'am. When you fall off a horse you got to get right back on. Mom won't let me ride until the cast comes off, but then I'm going to get right back on that horse."

"You remind me of Alec Ramsay."

"Who's he?"

"He's a boy a bit older than you but has your red hair and freckles. He has his very own horse."

"Wow, I wish I had my own horse."

"If I remember right, Alec spent the summer with his uncle who was a missionary in India. On returning home, his ship sank in a storm. Luckily for Alec, the ship had a wild horse on board. Both Alec and the horse were thrown overboard. Alec grabbed the rope tied around the horse's neck, and the horse pulled him to the safety of a small island. No one survived the shipwreck to claim the horse, so the horse became Alec's."

"Some people have all the luck. Nothing that exciting ever happens to me. Does Alec live around here?"

"Yes, I believe he does…Let me check."

Mrs. Weaver slowly walked over to one of the stacks as if each step inflicted considerable pain. I hadn't noticed that before. I assumed she had arthritis. A lot of old folks did. She returned with a book in hand, obviously for me—she had tricked me again.

"This is *The Black Stallion* by Walter Farley. I think you'll like it," she said. She gave me the book, which I was obliged to take. "Make sure you return it in two weeks."

"Yes, ma'am," I said.

I returned home with the book again hidden under my shirt and immediately took it to my room. Out of curiosity I flipped through the pages. Scattered among the sheets of prose were drawings in black ink. One showed a black horse rearing up on its hind legs. The horse had bulging muscles that rippled and gleamed like those of a prizefighter. He was sleek and mean looking, not the kind of horse that would tolerate a saddle.

I opened to the first page: *The tramp steamer Drake plowed away from the coast of India and pushed its blunt prow into the Arabian Sea...*I was on page 14 when my mother called me for dinner. The Drake was in a terrible storm and had been struck by lightning; it was beginning to sink. People were heading toward the lifeboats; the situation didn't look good.

After supper I asked to be excused so I could organize my baseball cards. It was not an unusual request; I often spent many hours with my baseball cards. I felt bad about the lie, but there was no way I could leave Alec in the middle of that storm with the ship sinking. I read well into the evening.

In the summer my parents let me stay up until ten o'clock. By then the Black Stallion had dragged Alec to a small deserted island, undoubtedly saving his life, but the Black Stallion was still a wild beast capable of killing Alec at any moment.

"Sean, time to turn off the lights."

I looked at the clock on my dresser. It was hard to believe it was already ten. I dog-eared my page and placed the book in its secure spot under my mattress. I turned off the light and lay in bed wondering how

Alec would survive on the island without food and water. Finally, I could endure no more. I found a flashlight in my closet and crawled under the covers so my parents wouldn't see my light shining on the ground from their bedroom window, and I read late into the night. When I awoke in the morning the batteries to my flashlight were dead. The book lay on the floor with a dog-ear marking the place I had stopped. I finished the book in two days.

I found Mrs. Weaver sitting at her desk as usual, the desk piled high with stacks of books. I placed *The Black Stallion* on a vacant spot on her desk. "I enjoyed the book," I said.

She looked up at me and smiled as if she knew I would. "He's quite the horse, isn't he."

"Even with his cut foot, he beat both Sun Raider and Cyclone. The race wasn't even close."

"He also won the Kentucky Derby," Mrs. Weaver added.

"No, ma'am," I said. "The race was in Chicago." I hated to correct her, but she was clearly mistaken.

"That was the race against Sun Raider and Cyclone. You don't think the Black Stallion stopped racing after Chicago, do you?"

She must have seen the confusion on my face. "Follow me," she said. She picked up The Black Stallion and headed toward the cornfield, walking slowly, obviously in pain. She stopped at an aisle labeled juvenile and headed down the row, stopping midway down the aisle. "These are the F's," she said. "The books are in alphabetical order by the author's last name. All these books were written by Walter Farley." She returned *The Black Stallion* to the stack.

I looked at the books in amazement. There were *The Black Stallion Returns*, *Son of the Black Stallion*, *The Black Stallion Revolts*, *The Black Stallion Mystery*. There must have been fifteen or more books in all.

"Walter Farley wrote a whole series about the Black Stallion." She pulled out *The Black Stallion Returns*. "This is the second book in the series."

"Can I read that one?" I asked.

She gave me the book. "Bring it back in two weeks."

I left the library with my treasure firmly gripped in my hands. I didn't care who saw me. I would read every one of the Black Stallion books; I had all summer. I finished reading The *Black Stallion Returns* in three days and returned for another book. Each time I read a book, Mrs. Weaver would quiz me about the story. I didn't need much encouragement; I was always willing to tell her about Alec's adventures.

Summer passed by too quickly. By late August I had read eight of the books. With two weeks left before school started, it seemed unlikely I would complete the series. Homework would make finding time for reading difficult. With *The Black Stallion Revolts* under my arm, I walked into the library. It was unusually quiet even for a library. I walked over to the main desk. Instead of Mrs. Weaver, a man in his late forties was sitting at her desk. I felt a bit of anger; he had no right to be there. That was Mrs. Weaver's desk.

"Where's Mrs. Weaver?" I demanded as if the man had personally hidden her away somewhere.

The man looked up at me paying particular attention to the red hair under my Detroit Tigers' baseball cap. "Mrs. Weaver died last night," he said, choosing his words carefully. "She had cancer, you know. She had been in a lot of pain."

I was overcome with shock. What the man was telling me couldn't be true. I wanted to run out of the library and never come back, but my feet wouldn't respond. I just stared at the man in disbelief.

"You must be Sean Connolly."

"Yes, sir."

"Mrs. Weaver spoke very highly of you." He reached into Mrs. Weaver's desk drawer and pulled out a package. It was wrapped in plain brown paper and had a card taped to the outside. "She wanted you to have this."

I thanked the man and quickly left the library; I didn't want anyone to see me cry, but I cried all the way home. I went straight to my room so my mother wouldn't see the tears in my eyes. I set the package on my bed, preferring not to open it as if opening the package would somehow confirm Mrs. Weaver's death. Then, I cried quietly for another ten minutes. She had given me a new life filled with fun and adventure, and now she had taken it away. It wasn't right.

The card attached to the package said simply, "Sean Connolly." I removed the card from the package—my mother always insisted I read the card first. I recognized Mrs. Weaver's meticulous handwriting. She wrote with a flourish that made me envious. My teachers always told me my handwriting left something to be desired.

"When you read this you will know that I am gone," she wrote. "Summer went by too quickly, but you made my last days enjoyable. Please don't cry for me. I am happy now, for I am Minnehaha the waterfall, and I must return to my homeland. I have gone to join my Hiawatha, and together we shall walk along the shores of Gitche Gumee by the shining Big-Sea-Water. If you come to visit, which I hope you do, you will find me in the mournful cry of the loon or the chirp of the cricket or the susurration of the gentle waterfall. I will be there for you."

I set the card aside, my eyes still filled with tears. I would never read another book without thinking of her. I knew what it was before I opened the package and pulled out the book. It was bound in aged brown leather and decorated with gold leaf. On the cover, printed in gold leaf, was—The Song of Hiawatha.

I caress the old leather binding with tired, arthritic fingers as I have done so many times in the past. Even with my eyes closed, I can identify every crease, every imperfection, as if such a book could have imperfections. The book has lost none of its magic over the years. Just holding it gives me an ineffable pleasure that even I cannot express in words.

Around me crickets are chirping, and down by the lake, a loon is voicing its lonely, mournful cry. The day is becoming cool. I feel a chill cut through my body, although a sheen of sweat covers my skin. I try to lift my hand to my throbbing head, but lack the strength. Vaguely I feel each heartbeat pounding within my chest, as adrenaline tries to compensate for the lack of glucose flowing in my blood. My heart races. It is a race it cannot win. My thoughts begin to fog. Where am I? I wonder. The crickets have ceased their chirping, as if to observe a moment of silence, and I can no longer hear the loon down by the lake. All I hear is the susurration of a gentle waterfall—and then there is silence.

Silent Night

Spider touches my shoulder and instantly I am awake. "It's two o'clock," he says.

I flick on a flashlight beneath my poncho and check my watch. Under the red light the dial on my watch confirms the time. It is not that I do not trust Spider, but it feels like I had just gotten to sleep. My watch begins at two. When my hour is up, I can return to sleep. Sleep is my escape from reality.

"Is anything going on?" I ask in a low whisper.

"Same-O, Same-O," he replies. "Nothing unusual."

"Did you do the radio check?"

"No."

Spider is wrapping himself in his poncho liner, showing no intention of making the call. I place the radio's receiver to my ear and key the mike.

"Sawbones 83 to Deadwood." I wait for a reply.

"Sawbones 83, this is Deadwood. Go ahead. Over."

"Sawbones 83 to Deadwood. How do you read us? Over."

"I read you lima charlie (loud and clear). Over."

"Sawbones 83…out."

I lean back against the trunk of a large bamboo tree and stare into the darkness. If they come, they will come from the front. Behind me large bamboo shoots rise up like thick prison bars. With a sharp machete one might make fifty feet an hour. No, if they come they will attack from the front where the land had once been cleared for farming. Tall grass has since reclaimed the clearing.

Spider is already breathing deeply in the early stages of sleep. War teaches one how to master sleep. Tonight I sleep in the grass at the edge of a bamboo thicket; two months ago it had been up against the still-warm foundation of a burned-out schoolhouse in downtown Pleiku—compliments of the Tet offensive.

I again stare into the darkness. Anything beyond ten feet is little more than a shadow. My mind drifts off to the real world. It is exactly twelve hours away. At home it is also two o'clock. My father will be getting out of work early. My mother would normally be working as a waitress at a local diner, but she will have the day off. I have a brother in the Peace Corps in Panama. There is no telling what he might be doing. Loneliness begins to set in. Back home

Christmas Eve is approaching. Over here every eve is the same.

"How can I be lonely with so many people around me?" you ask. "They are my friends," you say.

I am forced to acknowledge the wisdom of your argument. Around me are ten riflemen, a sergeant, and a newly minted second lieutenant. They are my friends. People back home assume we are fighting for our country—out of patriotism. What we fight for, when the bullets begin to fly, is not patriotism; it is for the guy in the foxhole beside us. That is what we fight for. It's as simple as that—nothing more. I will offer my life for the people beside me, as they will for me. Two days ago, before the recon patrol began, we had been strangers. I didn't even know their names. Now I do. One is named Spider, one is Juice, and we have a Tex. Every unit has a Tex. No matter what name I might have offered for myself, my name would be Doc. I am their medic. Those are all the names we need to know. Anything more is superfluous.

Perhaps loneliness is not the best term to express my feelings. Perhaps it is deeper than that—more a feeling of insignificance. I look above me. In a gap of the bamboo shoots I see a portion of the sky with its endless stars. The cleared area on the ground in front of me appears to zoom out like a cheap Hollywood movie stunt. It soon disappears, and the globe of the earth materializes. That too becomes smaller as the camera continues its outward zoom until the earth is only a speck, a small blue dot in some inconspicuous corner of the universe. I can now see myself from the viewpoint of the stars that have been shining down on earth for eternity.

"In the realm of the endless and eternal universe…do you believe a man sitting at the edge of a clearing with an M-16 in his lap really makes a difference?" the stars ask.

I can offer no reply.

In the sky that hangs loosely over the clearing are more stars. One of them is moving toward me. It has to be a plane or helicopter. At this time of night, it is more likely the former. A mile south of me, it begins to circle. I see the glowing, orange ribbon first. It looks like a streamer of crepe paper someone is waving in the night sky. But its fiery brilliance is breathtaking. Seconds later the sound reaches my ears. It is a low moan, like a painful wail from some mythical monster.

The Air Force calls them AC-47s, twin-engine planes equipped with three mini-guns each capable of spitting out 6,000 rounds a minute. Those of us unfortunate enough to have seen them in action from the ground called them "Spooky" or "Puff the Magic Dragon."

I watch the plane circle around spitting out its tracer fire. On the last round, it comes within 1,000 yards of our position. I key the mike on our radio.

"Sawbones 83 to Deadwood, over."

"Sawbones 83, this is Deadwood. Go ahead, over."

"Be advised we have Spooky at our doorstep. Does he know we're here? Does he have our coordinates? Over."

"Wait one, Sawbones 83…"

I visualize Deadwood back at base camp with his feet upon some desk. He will have a coffee mug in his left hand and will now be reaching for a sandwich with his right. After he has taken a couple of bites, he will pick up the landline and place a call to whoever is in charge of Spooky. It might not be fair, but that is the image lodged in my mind.

"Sawbones 83, this is Deadwood. Over."

"Deadwood, this is Sawbones 83. We're still here. We're not going anywhere."

"Be advised S-2 (military intelligence) has reason to believe Charlie is visiting your sector. Spooky was dispatched in your honor. When he leaves they'll place H and I rounds (harassment and interdiction) around your perimeter to keep Charlie honest."

"Roger that, Deadwood. Sawbones 83, out."

I hope my voice sounded calm and professional over the radio. It is not the way I feel. One small error and Spooky will be raining bullets down upon us like a summer hailstorm. Friendly fire won't even earn a purple heart. Does a wound from friendly fire hurt less? I wonder how well our lieutenant scored in his map-reading class at OCS.

I wait in the darkness, watching Puff do her thing. The ribbons of fire created by the tracers are almost a work of art as they lace through the night sky, but the moaning sound is unsettling, sending a chill through my body. It reminds me of the song *They Call the Wind Maria* from the musical *Paint Your Wagon*. How does that verse go?... "Maria makes the mountains sound like folks was out there dying."

"Is someone out there dying under that deluge of gunfire?" I wonder. Maybe no one will ever know.

"If someone in a woods cries out in pain and there is no one there to hear his cry, does he still suffer pain?" I ask.

"That's stupid," I reply. "The pain is just as real."

"Must you two always bicker?" a third voice says.

"Yes, we must," they reply in unison.

They are both right, of course—each in his own way. Somewhere, as I sit here in the dark, a woman is being raped. Not a sensual sex act, but a brutal, violent attack that is every bit as traumatic as anything this war has to offer. Somewhere, there is a young child suffering pain from the terminal stages of cancer. Somewhere, there is a mother or wife receiving a notice from a military chaplain. But I do not know them; therefore, they do not exist. They never happened.

"That is precisely the point I was trying to make," I say.

"But it's still real to the people involved," I reply.

It is obvious those two are not about to let it rest. I don't know why I put up with them. Spider doesn't suffer from such conflicts. He described his hour as "nothing unusual."

I lay my M-16 on the ground and reach into my rucksack for what remains of my dinner. It is a can of ham and lima beans from the C-ration pack. It has no commercial value, as it cannot be traded for anything. It is literally the bottom of the food chain, but when you're hungry, you'll eat anything. I open the can with my P-38 can opener and scoop out the contents with my plastic spoon. It isn't the tastiest meal, but it gives me something to do and prevents my mind from wandering.

I finish the beans with a polite, but subdued, burp and toss the can to the side. I will have to pick it up in the morning—nothing will be left to confirm our existence. By then it will be daylight. We will be able to see what we are doing.

I reach for my M-16 with my right hand —it isn't there. I am overtaken with panic. My heart races within my chest, and I begin to hyperventilate. With both hands I begin patting the ground. It only takes a moment or two to find the weapon, but my heart continues to race. I hold it close to my chest. I don't know why. My M-16 is still a virgin. I have never fired it in anger. Hopefully, I never will. Every time the fecal matter hits the proverbial fan, a medic is too busy to need a weapon. Still, it is my security blanket and I need it. I have dreams at night about losing my gun. Some people have dreams about having no clothes. I have dreams about having no gun. I am sure other people do not share such dreams. Sometimes I worry about my mental stability. Even emotionally stable people have cracked during wartime.

I clutch my M-16 to my chest like a mother clutching an infant just rescued from perilous danger;

then I feel foolish. I pull my poncho over my head and turn on my flashlight: it is two-thirty. My watch is half done.

I stare into the darkness for another ten minutes. In the darkness, there is nothing to see. With no wind, there is nothing to hear. Except for the lingering smell of ham and lima beans, there is nothing to smell. A university psychology department could not have constructed a better sensory-deprivation lab. It is good, but not perfect. About every five minutes, an artillery shell falls around our perimeter. They do provide more personal space than Spooky did; none fall closer than half a mile. No one in our squad is even awakened.

Those noises I can overlook. Those noises I can understand. What is disconcerting are the occasional noises in front of me. They are subtle to be sure, perhaps just my imagination. A lonely watch can do that to you. If someone else were present, the noise would qualify for a "Did you hear that?" Nothing more.

Sometimes the noises are real, but that does not make them sinister. Every land has its share of wildlife capable of creating noises in the night. I stare at the distant shadows—they appear to be moving. I rub my eyes and look again. Sometimes when there is no background for reference, objects appear to move. Psychologists call it auto-kinesis. The shadows continue to move. I focus on two shadows, paying particular attention to the space between them—the space remains constant. The movement is probably my imagination.

On the practical side, it would make no difference if they were real. We are a recon team. We are to avoid contact at all costs. We are motionless and silent. We have trees at our back, eliminating visible shadows. We will see them long before they see us.

What would happen if I did come face-to-face with my counterpart? Would I hesitate? Would he hesitate? Our country has been in many wars. All our old enemies are now our friends. Can I kill a man tonight who tomorrow could have been my friend? If I were to pretend I don't see him, would he pretend he doesn't see me and walk away?

I push my thoughts into the far recesses of my brain, but they are like articles of clothing in an over-stuffed suitcase—they resist closure.

I remain in place leaning against my bamboo backrest and give the chimerical bogey the right of passage. The next fifteen minutes are uneventful. I again crawl under my poncho to check the time: It is now five minutes to three; my watch is almost over. I key the mike on the radio. It is time for our hourly radio check.

"Sawbones 83 to Deadwood." There is no answer.

"Sawbones 83 to Deadwood." I again wait for a reply.

"Sawbones 83, this is Deadwood. Go ahead, over."

I can hear radio music in the background. Deadwood obviously does not get as much fresh air as we do.

"Sawbones 83 to Deadwood, how do you read us, over?"

"I read you lima charlie, over."

"Sawbones 83, out."

It should now be three o'clock. I crawl over to Juice and touch him on the shoulder. He is instantly awake.

"It's three o'clock…time for your shift," I whisper.

Juice rubs his eyes in hopes it will help him see into the darkness; it does not.

"Anything happen on your shift?" he asks.

"Same-O, Same-O," I reply, "Nothing unusual."

Three-Servicemen-statue overlooking the Wall

The Wall

I have been to the Wall
and have touched the cold granite.
Bleak in its blackness
on the mall it does stand
a reminder of the men
who died in that far away land.

I have been to the Wall
in search of a friend
I know not his name
nor does he mine
fore we met but a moment
in that far away land,

two ships in the night
both answered the call,
but his name alone
is etched on the Wall.

Does anyone remember
that carefree young man
snatched from our midst
in that far away land?

Does anyone remember
who knelt by his side,
who fought back the tears
the day that he died?

Does anyone remember
the hands drenched in blood
that cradled his head
as his life ebbed away,
there in the mud
on the ground where he lay?

Does anyone remember
that carefree young man
snatched from our midst
in that far away land?

I do.
Larry Buege Medic,
4th Infantry Div. 1967-68

God gave us memory
So we might have roses in December.
J. M. Barrie (1860–1937)

Alzheimer's Dementia is an insidious disease destined to affect as many as ten percent of our maturing population. For most of us, its social, emotional, and financial impact on family members is all too familiar. What we don't know, and may never know, is what transpires in the minds of those afflicted. Below is a short story from the viewpoint of an Alzheimer's patient. It is a work of fiction and represents one person's depiction of the disease Frozen Memories was the winner of *Marquette Monthly's* Annual Short-Story Contest in 2011

TITLE DEED

PARK PLACE

RENT $35.

With 1 House	$ 175.
With 2 Houses	500.
With 3 Houses	1100.
With 4 Houses	1300.

With HOTEL $1500.

Mortgage Value $175.
Houses cost $200. each

Hotels , $200. plus 4 houses

If a player owns ALL the Lots of any Color - Group the rent is Doubled on Unimproved Lots in that group.

Frozen Memories

I awake in a panic—this isn't my bedroom! Snapshots of happy families and small boys with baseball bats resting on their shoulders adorn the wall beside my bed, but I don't know these people and it scares me. What if they return and find me sleeping in their bed? I sit up in bed to make good my escape and discover someone has lashed me to the bed frame. Fear turns to rage, and I rip violently at the heavy canvas straps that tether my hips to the sides of the bed, but the straps refuse to yield. My screams mutate into deep growls and snarls that vent my frustration, although they offer no physical relief.

Then a strange woman wearing a yellow, flowery smock enters the bedroom.

"Good morning, John. It's Sally."

I glare at the woman. She has to be responsible for tying me to the bed. I hate her. If she comes closer, I can scratch her face or maybe bite her. She seems to understand my intentions and maintains her distance.

"Alice is coming to visit today. You don't want her to see you acting like this, do you?"

"I need to go home."

"Yes, of course you do. How could I forget?" she replies. "I believe I have your bus ticket right here." She reaches into the pocket of her smock and pulls out a small card. "Here's your bus ticket."

She gives me the ticket and then steps back. I carefully study the ticket. It says Park Place at the top. The ticket price is three hundred and fifty dollars. There is also information about hotels, which I ignore—I won't need a hotel; I'm going home.

"If we are going to get you to the bus stop on time, we need to get you dressed."

She helps me dress. She's a nice lady. "What is your name?" I ask.

"My name's Sally. Now let's get you into the wheel chair, so I can push you down to the bus stop."

She helps me onto my feet, but my legs cross and I can't separate them. She gives me a twist and I collapse into my wheelchair, my bus ticket firmly clinched in my hand.

"Alice will arrive around noon, so you can eat lunch with her."

I'll be on the bus before noon, but that's okay; I don't know Alice. The nice lady with the yellow smock rolls me through the double doors and into the sunlight. I wish I knew her name. She pushes the wheelchair along the sidewalk and then onto the newly mowed grass. The smell reminds me of the fresh-cut alfalfa of my youth. The lady rolls my wheelchair up to the end of a picnic table near two tall spruce trees. The table top was recently varnished, but bird droppings already decorate its surface.

"Is this yours?" I ask. I hold up the card in my right hand. "I don't know if this is any good."

"Yes, I believe that is mine," she says. "I've been looking all over for that." I give her the card. She seems happy and slips the card into her pocket.

"When Alice arrives, I'll bring your lunches, so you and Alice can have a picnic. Won't that be fun?"

I don't understand what she is saying and offer no reply. She leaves me in my wheelchair, alone with my thoughts; but I don't mind. I seldom get outside. A chickadee in the spruce tree scolds me for invading its space. It darts from branch to branch announcing its displeasure to all who will listen. Down below robins hop about on the lawn, pausing periodically to pull reluctant worms from the thick sod. The birds offer simple entertainment.

The kind lady soon returns with a woman in her mid-thirties. The young woman is dressed in a gray business suit, and I wonder if she is my doctor.

"Alice is here to visit with you," the kind lady says.

The young lady takes my right hand in both of hers and sits down at the picnic table. Her hands are soft and gentle and affectionately caress the back of my hand.

"How are you today?" she asks with a pleasant smile.

"I'm fine," I reply. "What's your name?"

"My name's Alice. I came to spend the afternoon with you."

She lets go of my hand long enough to retrieve a comb from her purse and run it gently through my gray hair. She's a nice lady. She places the comb back in her purse.

"Do you want a mint?" she asks. She finds a roll of mints in her purse and places one in her mouth. I open my mouth in anticipation. She takes another mint and places it on my tongue.

"Thank you," I say.

She sets the roll of mints on the picnic table and again takes my hand in her hands. It feels good. Her hands are so soft and smooth. I look down at my hands. They are rough and wrinkled with age, hardly worthy of her attention.

"What's your name?"

"My name's Alice."

She smiles at me. I wish she would come more often. I don't get many visitors. She's a very pretty lady.

"Do you live near here?" I ask.

"I live in Wexford. It's about one hundred and twenty miles south of here. I wish I lived closer. Then I could visit more often."

"I've never heard of Wexford." She has nice brown eyes, and when she smiles, her whole face smiles with her. "Do you come here often?"

"I was here last week."

"I wish you would have stopped by to see me."

"Do you remember Tommy? He's on a Little League team now. He says to tell you hello. I have a picture of him."

The young lady retrieves a snapshot from her purse and gives it to me. The picture shows a small boy with a bat at his shoulder smiling at the camera. His smile reminds me of the kind lady. I don't know the boy but nod anyway so as to not hurt the lady's feelings. He's a nice looking boy.

"Except for the dark hair, I think he looks like his grandfather." The lady places the picture back in her purse. "I want you to have the picture. I'll pin it on your bulletin board when we return to your room."

The kind lady from the nursing home returns with two food trays. She places one tray in front of me and gives the other to my lady friend. "Have you two been having fun?" she asks.

"We're having a good conversation," my lady friend replies. "I showed him a picture of Tommy, and I think he recognized him."

"You need to eat before everything gets cold," the kind lady says. "Today we have roast beef and mashed potatoes. John loves mashed potatoes and gravy."

I look at the mashed potatoes and my mouth begins to water. I hadn't realized how hungry I was. I take a spoon and scoop up some potatoes. My hand trembles and I miss my mouth. The gravy and potatoes drip down from my chin onto my shirt. Taking a napkin from my tray, the lady wipes my mouth and face. Then she gently pries the spoon from my hand. "Let me help," she says.

She takes some potato in the spoon and lifts it to my mouth. I open my mouth like a baby robin and remove the potato from the spoon with my tongue and upper lip. I like mashed potatoes with gravy. She continues to feed me until the food is gone, ignoring her tray. She is a nice lady.

"What's your name?" I ask.

"My name's Alice," the young woman replies. She again wipes my face with a napkin. "Do you want to go for a walk?" I nod my head in the affirmative.

The young lady takes the rolls from the two trays and places them in her pocket. Then she releases the brakes on the wheelchair and pushes me back to the sidewalk. "We can walk over to the pond and feed the ducks."

The duck pond is at the edge of the nursing home property. It is only a small stream that has been dammed up to form a half-acre pond, but the ducks don't seem to care. About ten ducks are floating on the pond while another five or six are sitting on the grass at the edge of the pond. The young lady pushes my wheelchair close to the water's edge where a park bench overlooks the pond. She sits down beside me on the bench.

"Do you remember how to feed the ducks?" she asks. She breaks apart one of the rolls and hands a fragment to me. The ducks seem to understand and immediately gather at my feet. A mother duck and eight small ducklings wait patiently farther back.

"Throw them the bread," my lady friend tells me. I throw the piece of bread, and it falls not far from my feet. The ducks converge upon it in a flurry of feathers. She gives me another piece of bread. The ducks are now quacking noisily in anticipation. I throw out the bread, and they again fight over the small morsel. I feel sad that the young ducklings don't catch any of the bread. The third piece I throw directly to them, and one of the ducklings grabs the bread. He is immediately chased by his siblings. It makes me smile. I can't remember when I had such fun.

The young woman is laughing at me or maybe she is laughing at the ducklings. I'm not sure which. I like laughter. I'm glad she came to visit.

"You're a nice lady," I tell her. "If I ever have a daughter, I hope she's just like you."

The young woman smiles, but it is a forced smile. Her dark brown eyes—the ones I had found so filled with joy—slowly well up with water until a solitary tear cascades over her left check. She makes no attempt to wipe it away.

"Why are you crying?" I ask.

Troubled Waters

"We have to leave," I said. "The river's rising." Standing in two feet of water, I was explaining the obvious.

The woman stared at me as if she did not hear. Judging by a few gray roots in her otherwise brown hair, I assumed she was in her late thirties or early forties. Not all her hair was gray, just enough to justify trips to the hairdresser. She did not bother to introduce herself nor did I. My name was embroidered on my fatigue jacket if she really needed to know. This was day three with little sleep, and I no longer cared whom I was rescuing. She was one more warm body, one more piece of baggage to load into my johnboat and drag back to the armory for three squares and a cot. Someday—when I look back through the warped prism of time—I may remember my actions as passionate, perhaps even heroic. Today, I only want to sleep. The sky was dull and opaque, giving no indication of time; although my watch confirmed the lateness of the day. By the time the woman joined the host of other refugees, it would be too dark for further rescue efforts. Then I could sleep.

The current was mild in the two feet of water in which I now stood, but the drag on the johnboat strained against the rope I held. The boat was painted in a confusion of greens intended to render the boat invisible, but it looked silly against the brown river water. The only identifying mark was the battalion designator painted on the bow. I pushed the boat against the front porch where the woman stood ankle-deep in water. She had her jeans rolled up to her knees, but they were still wet. Behind her, through the open door, I could see water covering a brown thick-piled carpet. It might have been a different color on a different day, at a different time. Now it was ruined. There was no way to remove the mud and silt that would remain after the river receded, providing the house was still standing. The current had eroded much of the foundation, and the house was on the verge of collapse. I assumed it would be gone by morning.

"Ma'am, do you need help getting into the boat?" I asked.

My question was met with silence. The woman stared into the distance as if discerning some speck on the horizon, but her eyes transmitted no images to her brain. I had seen it before—during the war. Educated people called it the *thousand-yard stare*. The rest of us called it shell-shock, burn out…hitting the wall. The woman's brain was in sensory overload and blocking further input. It was the equivalent of an ostrich inserting its head into the sand in hopes the world would go away. If her brain were a computer, we would say it crashed and needed rebooting. Other than her upright posture, the only evidence of life was the slow undulating motion of her hands as she washed away imaginary stains. Her fingers were chaffed from long hours of physical labor. Large veins protruded from the backs of her hands. They were covered with skin thinned with middle age. Perhaps she was older than I had originally presumed, or maybe life's misfortunes had aged her prematurely. I really didn't care. I had a job to do. I needed sleep.

"Ma'am, we need to leave. The river's washing away your house. It's no longer safe." I said it louder than need be. It was almost a yell, but it got her attention. She looked at me as if she had seen me for the first time. "Your house can't last much longer. It's washing away. We need to leave."

"I have to stay with my quilt. I can't leave my quilt. My husband gave it to me." She spoke softly, almost a whisper. Her voice was void of inflection and emotion, and she refused to look at me as if she were talking to someone else.

I looked at her hand and found a simple wedding band. I don't know why I hadn't noticed it earlier. "Where's your husband?"

"He left to find work. He's coming back. I promised to care for the quilt until he returns. He gave me the quilt."

"You won't need the quilt. I'm taking you to the armory. They'll have cots and warm blankets and hot soup. You won't need the quilt."

"I can't leave my quilt." She looked at me as if I were the one insane.

The rain had stopped, but it was only temporary. I looked up at the sky, which remained uniformly gray and shapeless. I could see no clouds, but I knew they were there, somewhere above me. That could be three hundred feet or three thousand feet. There was no sense of depth, just grayness.

If I were physically capable, I would have carried her to the boat just to get on with it, but I couldn't steady the boat and carry a struggling adult even if it was a woman. She was breaking no laws. I had no right to force her into my boat.

"Ma'am, where's your quilt? If I get your quilt will you leave with me?"

"I can't leave my quilt. My husband gave it to me. I promised I would care for the quilt."

"What does the quilt look like?"

"It's very pretty. It's pink and soft and cuddly. My husband gave it to me."

With the water eroding the foundation, I couldn't leave her. The woman and her house would be gone by morning. Neither could I waste time. There were others in need. The johnboat had no oars or motor and was meant to be towed. That was fine when the water was low, but there were already areas waist deep in water, and the force of the current was increasing. The river wouldn't crest for another two days. I needed to leave now.

"Wait here. I'll get your quilt."

"I can't leave my quilt."

I tied the johnboat to the porch railing, hoping it would hold. The woman, oblivious to my actions, returned to her thousand-yard stare, tuning reality out of her sphere of consciousness. I headed into the house. It stunk with the odor of damp mold. The electricity had been out for two days, and the house was dark even though the sun, somewhere beyond the storm clouds, had yet to set. I turned on my flashlight and began a search for anything pink and resembling cloth. It occurred to me that its existence was in doubt. I found nothing on the ground floor, but a foot of water now covered the floor. If the woman had left the quilt on the floor, I would never find it. Leading off from what had been a living room was a staircase. The railing was still intact. Even in the dim light, I could appreciate the fine craftsmanship of the cherry woodwork. At one time—perhaps last week— this had been an attractive home. I started up the steps and found them solid although warped from the listing of the house. If I didn't find the quilt during a cursory exam of the bedrooms, I would leave—with or without the woman.

The bedrooms were capacious and decorated with a feminine touch. Pictures of landscapes hung on the walls. Lacy curtains, now soggy and smelling of mold, draped the windows. In the first room—I assumed to be the master bedroom—I found a wedding picture taken not many years ago. A woman dressed in a white wedding gown stood in front of a late model car, smiling up at her new husband. I studied the picture for a moment before convincing myself that the bride in the picture was the same woman now standing in six inches of water on the front porch. Maybe she was not as old as I had thought, or perhaps she married late in life. She looked happy, ready to take on the world—how quickly our dreams shatter.

The second room was smaller but still large by most standards. A double bed made up and prepared for company was the cynosure of the room. The bedspread was hand embroidered in reds and yellows, but that was not what drew my attention. Lying wadded up on the bed was a pink quilt. It looked soft and cuddly, as the woman had described. This, too, appeared hand embroidered—not a typical store-bought gift a husband would buy. I had assumed the quilt, if found, would be neatly folded consistent with its obsessive-compulsive owner; but then, she was a study in inconsistencies. I scooped up the quilt and prepared to leave. It was heavy—too heavy for a quilt. I peeled away the layers of quilt until I stared into the inquisitive gray-blue eyes of a young infant—the gift from her husband.

*Foreign Policy

Somewhere in Uniqueastan

The kerosene lamp sitting on a rock ledge provided minimal illumination, creating grotesque shadows on the wall of the cave. The cave was small but provided adequate shelter from the elements. The two men sitting cross-legged on the floor facing each other did not appear concerned about their humble surroundings. Both men wore turbans and robes common to the locale. A small fire licked at the carcass of a large rodent, extracting the natural juices, which dripped onto the fire creating puffs of yellow flame.

"Ain't that C-4 you're burning?" asked one of the men in a heavy accent, obviously a Uniqueastanian.

"Yep," replied the other in perfect English. A large wart perched on the tip of his nose invited comment, but his menacing eyes dissuaded all but the fool hardy.

"Ain't that plastic explosive?"

"Yep." The man with the wart cut a piece of meat from the rodent with a large knife, elevating it to his mouth with the blade. "Care for a piece?" the man asked the Uniqueastanian.

"I'll pass." The Uniqueastanian stared at the burning plastic explosive with unconcealed concern. "You sure burning C-4 is safe?"

"Yep." The man with the wart ripped a leg off the carcass and placed the entire leg in his mouth. He skinned all meat from the bone with his teeth and tossed the bone to the side of the cave. A large pile of lizard bones and snake heads confirmed that he had resided in the cave for several days. "Do it all the time. Long as there's no blasting cap, it only burns." The Uniqueastanian did not appear convinced.

"I understand your country might be interested in a major purchase." The Uniqueastanian caressed his AK-47 that lay on the ground by his side. He always liked to know where it was during delicate negotiations.

"Depends on what ya got." The man with the wart had a fully loaded Uzi submachine gun resting comfortably in his lap; however, he preferred his knife at such close quarters, should a difference of opinion develop. He tossed the rest of the roasted rodent into the corner; maggots could have the leftovers. He wiped his greasy mouth on his sleeve and waited for the Uniqueastanian to elaborate.

"How about a twenty-megaton nuclear bomb. Not too big but can still make a mess. Got it from a Soviet army surplus store. Sort of a going out of business sale."

"Does it come with a missile?"

"Short-range, ballistic missile. Range about sixty miles, but that'll cost you extra."

"My government would be interested in removing some of these toys from the playground. How much you want?"

"One billion Yankee dollars and ten virgins."

"One billion Yankee dollars and ten virgins!" Nostrils began to flare, and the American's eyes became wide as if suddenly infused with drugs. The Uniqueastanian reached for his AK-47 but was too late. A heavy foot came down hard on the weapon, pinning it to the ground. Subtle motions with the large knife discouraged further aggressive behavior, and the Uniqueastanian released his grip on the rifle.

"You people think America has unlimited assets, that all you have to do is ask your exorbitant price and it will automatically flow out of the land of milk and honey. American opulence has boundaries. Our resources are not inexhaustible. We can't always give in to your greed just because you ask."

The American looked over his nose, past the warty protuberance, and into the eyes of the, now quivering, Uniqueastanian. "Would you consider one billion Yankee dollars and five virgins?"

"Deal."

Flying High

Matt Pippin opened the window of his Ford pickup and crushed his cigarette stub on the truck's rusted-out frame. With a flick of his finger, he sent the cigarette butt into the brush alongside the trail. It had rained the day before, and the ground was still damp, eliminating any threat of fire—at least that was how he rationalized his behavior.

The trail—two parallel ruts through the woods—led north off M-28 into the Hiawatha National Forest. It no longer provided any commercial value and was used only by hunters and dirt-bikers—and then only rarely. Matt returned both hands to the wheel to fight through a section of ruts that made steering difficult. Four-wheel drive was not obligatory, but few people ventured down the trail without it. The high ground-clearance of the pickup, however, was mandatory to avoid the protruding rocks.

Matt reached over and relieved Jennifer of the paper-bag-wrapped bottle. He didn't know if it were true, but he had heard cops couldn't bust you for "in possession" unless they could see the bottle—not without a search warrant. He raised the bottle to his lips and took a swig.

"Take it easy on that stuff," Jen said. "This isn't the best road to drive drunk."

"Relax; I'm just drinking enough to mellow me out. I have no intention of getting drunk…stoned, maybe, but not drunk."

Matt passed the bottle back to Jen who took a sip and then wedged the bottle between her thighs to free both hands. She placed her left hand behind Matt's neck and let her fingers creep up into his dark brown hair. She took a drag on the cigarette held in her right hand and coughed out white smoke. She had not yet become accustomed to smoking. Matt eased off the accelerator when he came to a puddle in the road left by the previous day's rain. It was about ten feet across, hopefully not deep. It wasn't necessary, but Matt punched the pickup into four-wheel drive. He stepped on the gas, gunning the truck across the water.

"How much farther is it?" Jennifer asked.

"It's twelve miles from the highway. We got about a mile to go." Minutes later, the trail opened into a clearing.

"That's it," Matt said.

Grass, grown wild over the years, covered most of the clearing. Here and there, half-buried iron pipes, rusty flywheels, and remnants of old steam engines protruded from the sod. A tall structure framed with thick timbers and covered by gray, weathered planks rose almost fifty feet from the center of the clearing. It housed the shaft of the Sage Iron Ore Mine.

Painsdale Copper Mine

Built in the early twenties, it had never turned a profit and was abandoned after five years of operation. Iron ore was abundant in many areas of the Upper Peninsula—this was not one of them.

Matt drove around the structure to ensure they were alone, and then parked behind the building under some trees.

"Looks creepy," Jen said. "Are you sure it's safe?"

"Been up there several times, and it hasn't fallen down yet." Although not intoxicated, Matt had reached that mellowness he had been striving for. He placed the bottle of wine in his school backpack along with a cheap digital camera. "Come on, let's go. It's a beautiful view from up there. Maybe we can get some good pictures. In an hour or so, there should be a decent sunset."

A rusty, nineteen-twenties padlock secured the door to the structure. It was a needless gesture. Matt led Jennifer to a section of the wall where several boards were missing. They stepped inside and waited until their eyes adjusted to the dim light. The inside was dark and damp and smelled of mold, but enough light leaked through the cracks between the wooden planks to outline the remaining carcass of the old mine hoist. The county sealed the mineshaft years ago for safety reasons, but left intact the iron girders and pulleys that raised and lowered the ore carts. They still reached up to the top of the fifty-foot structure.

"There's a small room at the top." Matt took Jennifer's hand and led her to a set of wooden stairs without risers that switch-backed up the far wall. Normally, Jennifer would have been reluctant, but she had also mellowed out on the wine and followed Matt up the creaking stairs without comment.

When Matt reached the top, he pushed up on a trap door providing entry to a twelve-by-fifteen-foot room. Rusty beer cans and broken wine bottles were testimony that they were not the first individuals to use the room.

Matt pushed open two swinging doors, and sunlight flooded into the room. Jennifer backed away. Even with a modest amount of alcohol running through her veins, she had sufficient prudence to shy away from the fifty-foot drop. "They used these doors to bring in heavy equipment," Matt said. "It's a pretty view, isn't it?" The leaves on the trees had unfurled their spring plumage revealing rolling hills of green for as far as they could see. Matt opened his backpack and had a sip of wine, and then he took several pictures from the open doorway.

"Not so close to the edge, Matt. You make me nervous."

Matt stepped back from the door and removed the rest of the backpack's contents. He looked admiringly at a Ziploc sandwich bag with some white crystals at the bottom. He had paid a good sum of money for those crystals. Another bag contained brown, shredded leaves.

Jennifer took a sip of the wine. "That's it?" she asked as she examined the bag of white crystals.

"Twenty grams of high purity methcathinone, the big Cat."

"How long does it last?" Jen asked with mild interest.

"Depends on how you use it. A needle gives you the best rush but doesn't last long. Snorting provides a milder high that lasts a little longer."

"I'm not using any needles."

"Don't have to. We're going to mix it with the marijuana and smoke it."

"How do you know so much about drugs?" Jen asked.

"The Internet—the *Partnership for a Drug-Free America* has a good website."

"What does it feel like?"

"I've only tripped a couple of times, but it gives you a feeling of euphoria, almost like a mental orgasm. You feel like you're floating in air. It gives you endless strength."

"Is it dangerous?"

"It'll make your heart race. People with heart problems have died, but it's safe if you're young and healthy."

"It's still sounds creepy. What if I have a bad trip?"

Matt mixed some of the Cat with the dried marijuana and wrapped it in cigarette paper. "We'll go one at a time. I'll let you go first. I won't take a drag until I know you're not having a bad trip."

Matt raised the supercharged cigarette to his lips and held a match to the tip. He inhaled slowly until the tip glowed red. Then he passed it to Jennifer. "Here, just suck slowly on this and hold your breath as long as you can. It'll give the drug more time to enter your system."

Jen took a drag on the cigarette and held her breath as suggested. After three inhalations, a warm sensation swept through her body. She sat back and giggled. "I feel weird."

"Do you like it?"

"It's sort of neat. But everything is blurry."

"That's because the drug dilates your pupils."

Jennifer closed her eyes, eliminating the blurred vision, which she found pleasantly irritating. She could see much better with her eyes closed; her imagination filled the voids. "I could do this all day."

"Unfortunately, this is all I have. That stuff's not cheap."

"Where'd ya get it?"

"Don't ask. Let's just say I have a friend who can supply all the cocaine, Cat, and marijuana I'll ever need."

"I have ways to make you talk," Jennifer giggled. With eyes still closed, she stood up and began spinning around the room with arms out to her sides like a ballerina. Exotic music, seemingly coming from nowhere, flowed effortlessly from synapse to synapse in the depths of her brain. The beat was intense, constantly increasing in tempo and rhythm. They were playing her song. In a state of ecstasy, she danced around the ballroom, swaying from side to side, while admiring peasants threw rose petals at her feet.

"Careful you don't waltz out the opening," Matt said. "It's a long way to the ground."

"I don't care."

Matt pushed her back when she got close to the opening. After five minutes, Jen's high began to taper. Finally, the music withered and died. Jen sat down in the far corner of the room, a smile still on her face. "That's neat stuff. Can we do it again?"

"I'm next." Matt took a drag on a cigarette heavily laced with Cat. "I'm going to see if I can get a stronger high." He felt a rush but continued inhaling the fumes. This would be his best high yet. After several minutes, the cigarette fell from his hands. The euphoria was overwhelming. He had reached a level he had never before obtained. His feet were weightless, and he floated effortlessly across the room. His energy was without limit. He could leap over tall buildings in a single bound. He was faster than a speeding bullet. Nothing could stop him. He was Superman. He could fly!

Then he heard it: voices. "Someone's coming!"

"I don't hear anyone," Jennifer said.

"Can't you hear the voices?" Beads of sweat clung to Matt's forehead; and his eyes, now fully dilated, had a glazed appearance.

"Stop it, Matt. You're scaring me." But Matt was no longer listening—not to her.

"We got to get out of here."

"Okay, let's go back to the truck." Jen took Matt's hand, pulling him toward the staircase.

"No, not that way. We can't go that way. They're coming up the steps. Don't you hear them? They're coming after us. We need to get out of here. We have to go out this way." Matt headed toward the opening.

"No, Matt!"

"We can do it. We can float to the ground. We can fly."

"Matt, no!"

Matt spread his wings and soared through the opening, flying all the way to the ground. Jennifer heard no scream or cry for help, only a thud like a bag of feed hitting the ground.

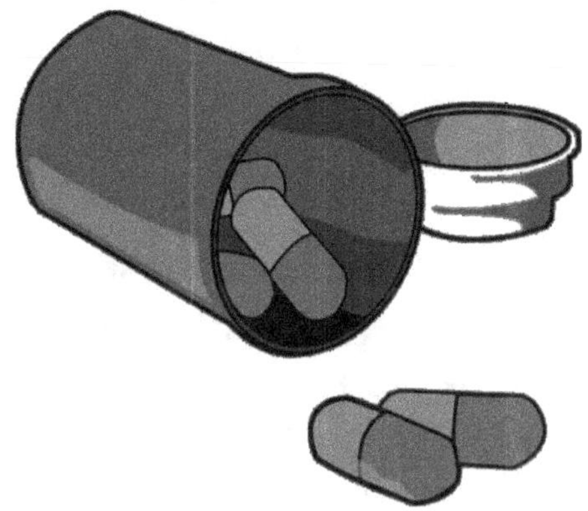

A Difficult Decision

"What's that?" Tammy asked. Sitting on her dinner plate next to the punctiliously placed napkin and silverware was a self-sealing bag containing fragments of dried leaves mixed with a few small seeds. The crumpled leaves had turned grayish brown with age, but like a fine wine had lost none of its value in the process. Drying the leaves had only concentrated the desirable biological resins making the merchandise all the more potent. Including the bag, it only weighed two ounces, but it was top of the line.

"I thought we might start the meal with a tossed salad. Maybe it will give us something to talk about." Karla Dykstra sat facing her thirteen-year-old daughter at the dinner table wondering where the conversation would take them. This was as far as she had planned the confrontation. From this point on, she had been hoping for divine guidance or perhaps a bit of spontaneous inspiration; none was forthcoming.

Motherhood wasn't supposed to be an endless confrontation between parent and child; yet, over the last two years, the quality time between Karla and her daughter had degenerated into a weekly testing of wills. Her degree in elementary education had not prepared her for such encounters. Her expertise was with seven-year-olds. Those she could handle. She would gladly take twenty unruly second-graders over one moody teenager capable of transforming the most mundane conversation into an ugly scene replete with uncontrollable emotional outbursts and pointless rantings. A rational discussion with her teenage daughter was asking a lot these days. It would have been easier if her father were here.

"You broke into my room and went through my things? What ever happened to privacy?"

Tammy's reply evinced anger, noticeable only by the tremor in her voice and a tightening of facial muscles that made the small birthmark on her upper lip quiver. Karla had seen that quivering lip frequently over the past several months—too frequently. Tammy could project a good front—as if she were in control of the situation—but the quivering lip always gave her away.

"I don't rummage through *your* damn stuff. I respect *your* privacy. Why can't you respect mine?"

"For your information, little lady, you happen to be *my* daughter and your room happens to reside in *my* house." Karla hoped her voice was calm. The line between firm and argumentative was thin. She had a habit of crossing that line when her patience was challenged. "You may think you're the cute little princess, but I'm still the queen, and I'll go through your room any time I please until you earn my trust."

Karla waited for a response, but was met with silence typical of her daughter's passive-aggressive behavior. Given a preference, Karla would have preferred an emotional outburst, anything that would qualify as a response. But her daughter had signaled the end of the discussion and was now staring vapidly at her plate as if the bag of marijuana no longer existed.

As was her habit under stress, Tammy twirled her right index finger around a strand of naturally blond hair that hung well below her shoulders—too long for Karla's taste. If truth were known, Tammy *was* a princess. At age thirteen she already had a model's figure that could pass for sixteen. And despite her poor grades, she was not the stereotypically dumb blond. Karla had no doubt Tammy could bring home straight A's with minimal effort if she were to apply herself. Unfortunately, academic activities were spurned in the pursuit of social acceptance. The desire for popularity dominated Tammy's existence. This was where she excelled. With her sharp wit and ingratiating conversational skills, she easily made friends. It was the integrity of those friends that concerned Karla.

"You promised you wouldn't do drugs anymore," Karla said, unwilling to let the matter rest. "Sooner or later you'll be caught by someone who may not be as understanding and forgiving. That won't be a pleasant experience for either of us."

"It's only a little pot. Give me some credit. I have enough sense to stay away from the heavy stuff."

"What's this then…vitamin pills?" Karla tossed a pill bottle toward her daughter. It rolled across the table coming to a stop next to Tammy's plate.

"I think it's like *speed*. It clears the mind and helps me with my homework. They're not harmful."

"You *think* it's speed? You're taking drugs, and you don't even know what they are? At least you're not overdosing on them. With your recent grades, your mind can't be too clear." Karla regretted her words before they left her lips. Sarcasm was never helpful. Her frustration should not dictate the course of the conversation. "What would your father say?"

"He's not going to say anything," Tammy replied, her anger now palpable. "In case you haven't noticed, he's not here. He's not coming back. Remember that man we buried three years ago? The guy filled with cancer? Remember him? That was your husband. My father's gone. He's dead. Live with it."

"Tammy, that's no way to talk about your father."

"I'll say anything I want about my father. He's no longer a part of this family. Maybe smoking a little weed would do *you* some good. Maybe it'll help *you* accept his death."

Karla paused to collect her emotions. The truth was she did have trouble accepting Chad's death. Life had been simple while Chad was alive.

"Tammy, I love you too much to watch you destroy your life like this. For the next month you'll remain in the house, except for school. You may have friends over only when I'm home. If you can bring your grades up, I'll reconsider."

"*Pleeese*…Give me a break. You don't love me. I'm just an embarrassment to your middle-class values, an inconvenient speed bump in your precious social life. Admit it: You hate me and I hate you."

"I don't hate you, Tammy."

Breaking into tears, Tammy stood up and threw the bag of marijuana at the wall, bringing the conversation to its ineluctable conclusion. "Well, I hate you! I wish you weren't my mother." Tammy kicked at her chair causing it to fall against the table. A second kick sent it tumbling to the floor. Satisfied that she had won her battle against the chair, Tammy ran to the sanctuary of her bedroom and slammed the door behind her.

With Tammy's departure, the dining room became engulfed in silence. Karla sat alone at the dinner table watching steam rise from the neglected meatloaf. Her three-bedroom ranch on the north side of Grand Rapids now seemed so empty, exacerbating Karla's feeling of loneliness. There had never been such silence when Chad was alive. Parties were frequent and boisterous. When not entertaining friends, there was always someone watching TV or bouncing a basketball on the driveway. Evening meals were accompanied by pleasant discussions, not acrimonious altercations. They were a real family, three musketeers: one for all and all for one. Perhaps the relationships were not totally equal; Tammy had been a daddy's girl. In Tammy's eyes, he could do no wrong. Chad had an ineffable charisma that charmed girls of all ages. At times, Karla was almost jealous. Then Chad would scoop her up in his strong arms, and she would be putty in his hands. Maybe that was what made his death so painful, watching such a strong man waste away. The cancer was inoperable when they found it—lung cancer and he didn't even smoke. They gave him chemotherapy, but all it did was destroy his beautiful brown hair and sap what remaining strength he still possessed. Pain was constant and relentless despite the medication. Just before he died, he was down to one hundred and twelve pounds of ribs and excess skin. His eyes had sunken into their sockets like some hideous Hollywood ghoul. That dying man was not the man she married. As Karla became more depressed, Chad became more upbeat, as if he needed to endure the pain for both of them. What hurt him the most—even more than the cancer—was when Tammy refused to visit him in the hospital. He said he understood her feelings, but Karla sensed his pain.

After Chad's death, Karla's friends—finding no niche in social circles for a single mom—drifted away. She still spoke to them occasionally at church or the supermarket, but they no longer shared anything in common. That was when Tammy began to drift away. Karla had been hoping it was a teenage phase Tammy would outgrow. At the moment that did not look promising.

Karla considered eating a slice of the meatloaf while it was still warm, then decided against it. The meatloaf would have to be resurrected on another day. Her appetite was gone, and it was unlikely Tammy would venture out of her bedroom before morning. In cases like this, Karla had found it best to give Tammy some space, at least for now. Tomorrow—when, hopefully, Tammy would be in a better mood—the subject could be revisited.

Who was she kidding, Karla wondered. Tomorrow, Tammy would be the same surly Tammy as today. Tammy was never in a better mood *tomorrow*. The truth was Karla was not up to further confrontation with Tammy. Postponing the confrontation was for her benefit, not Tammy's.

Karla cleared the table and washed the dishes. She resisted the temptation to clean house; that was what she normally did when angry. There were times when she almost vacuumed holes in her rug venting her anger. Tonight, she was rapidly approaching that point. She retrieved the bag of marijuana and placed it on the table next to the pills. She didn't know why. The room seemed tidier with the drugs in some semblance of order.

Karla stared at the contraband lined up on the table. The marijuana would have to be destroyed; the pills she could take to the drugstore for identification, not that it would make any difference. It surely didn't make any difference to Tammy; she used the pills on faith alone. Tears filled Karla's eyes and then cascaded down her checks. She cried until the tears no longer flowed. Then, she wiped them dry with Kleenex. Tomorrow was no longer an option: this could not wait.

Karla was not surprised to find Tammy's bedroom door closed: Tammy cherished her privacy. Karla knocked on the door twice with no response; then she opened the door and stepped into the room. "We need to talk."

"You've said everything. There's nothing more to say." Tammy lay on her bed facing the wall, feigning interest in a magazine. She was not about to make it easy. Karla did not find that surprising.

"This has to stop." Karla paused hoping for a response, but heard none. "When the police catch you—and they will, they'll refer you to social services…assuming you're not arrested." Tammy continued staring at her magazine, giving no indication that she had heard—except for the quivering lip. "The people at social service won't play your silly games," Karla continued. "They'll take your behavior seriously. Neither you nor I will call the shots once they're involved. You could be placed in a foster home for two or three months with rules far stricter than you have here." Karla again paused waiting fruitlessly for some reaction. "Is that what you want?"

Tammy put down her magazine and looked at her mother for the first time. "If you're worried about embarrassment, you can relax; the police won't catch me. I don't store drugs at school or carry them with me, and the police need probable cause to search the house. After tonight, you can rest assured they won't find anything in *your* house. I'll keep everything outside."

"After tonight you won't have access to *outside*. You may call it house arrest or whatever suits your fancy, but you're not leaving this house."

"You going to put bars on the windows? I can crawl out my window whenever I want. In fact, I may be out late tonight. Don't bother waiting up for me."

"Drug pushers do it for the money. What are you going to use for money? You're going to be hard pressed to find two coins in your pocket to jingle. I'll buy your lunch tickets, and if you need anything else, let me know and I'll make the purchase for you. Without an allowance or other money, there'll be no drugs. Do I make myself clear?"

"There're ways a girl can earn spending money."

Karla knew Tammy was right. Tammy had a figure that could easily be traded for cash. She had already learned the attention-getting value of a tight-fitting sweater. Her youth would only increase the value of her merchandise.

Karla returned to the dining room, placed a CD in the stereo, and sat at the table. Despite efforts of restraint, more tears began to flow. She was not normally a crier. She hadn't even cried when Chad died. Maybe Tammy was right. Maybe she hadn't accepted her husband's death. She still felt like Chad would some day come bouncing through the door with a smile on his face. If he were here, the two of them would surely find a solution to Tammy's behavior. When they worked together, insurmountable problems did not exist. But Chad was not here. He would not come bouncing through the door to save the day.

Karla picked up the bag of marijuana and the amber bottle of unlabeled pills. The marijuana might be no worse than alcohol, but even alcohol can be potent for a thirteen-year-old. What she worried about was the pills. Tammy didn't even know what they were. Terry Barton's daughter overdosed two years ago. As far as Karla knew, the police never caught Terry's daughter with any drugs—not until they found her body in that abandoned warehouse surrounded by empty pill bottles. Tammy was as street-wise as Terry's daughter. The odds of the police catching Tammy were remote.

The stereo played softly in the background. She had chosen a CD of ballroom dance music for its soothing effect. Chad liked ballroom dancing. That was how they met: at a college dance class. She had wanted nothing more than a no-sweat phys. ed. class. Instead, she was swept off her feet by a tall, slender engineering student. Shining armor could not have made him more enticing. The stereo faded as the current piece came to its end and segued into the "Blue Danube." That was Chad's favorite waltz. Karla closed her eyes and allowed Chad to waltz her around their living room. His hand felt strong against her back as he guided her through the steps. After a few minutes, the waltz faded into a slow dance. Chad pulled her close, pressing Karla's breasts against his chest. Karla placed her chin on his right shoulder and leaned her face against his. She could smell his aftershave. It was English Leather; he never wore anything else. The hand on her back slowly slid up until his fingers were combing through her hair. She felt so strong in his arms. If only he were real.

"I *am* real," he said.

"But only until I open my eyes," Karla replied. "I'm so alone. I wish you were here to help me."

Slowly, they danced across the floor. When the music was about to end, Chad placed his lips next to her ear and whispered, "Karla, you don't need my help…you know what to do."

"Yes," she said. "I do."
"It will be painful," Chad said.
"I know," she replied.
"Do it."

The music faded, and Karla opened her eyes—he was gone. All that remained was the faint smell of English Leather. Karla wiped her eyes dry, picked up the phone, and dialed 9-1-1.

*Amateur Skunk Removal 101

Warning: The following procedure was performed by a professional novice with years of inexperience. Please do not try this at home.

The United States Constitution guarantees the right to bear arms in defense of home and by extension, garden. With that mandate, I began trapping trespassers of all colors and stripes in the summer of 2008. By July 4th, I had bagged four gophers and two snowshoe hares. On the morning of July 6th, I was confronted with this black intruder with white racing stripes. I had to assume he was armed and dangerous. Removal of this biological time bomb with WMD capability had to be conducted with utmost caution. With the possibility of poisonous gas, I longed for my National Guard MOPP (Mission Oriented Protective Posture) gear.

The Equipment

It is imprudent to proceed without the proper equipment. The equipment I used consisted of an old Army poncho, a telescoping pole with hooked tip, and duct tape (not shown). The inquisitive skunk is watching the preparation from his live trap. According to the Internet (which is never wrong), skunks can shoot their stinky spray up to fifteen feet. The telescoping pole is ten feet long.

The Pre-wrap

I lifted the live trap with the hook at the end of the ten-foot pole. The skunk appeared nervous, but held his fire. I then placed the trap in the center of the poncho. Everything looks good, Mission Control. The retro-rockets have not been deployed.

Gift Wrapped

Using the ten-foot pole, I flipped the sides of the poncho over the trap. Once the trap was covered, I was able to move in to strap the poncho down with duct tape. As long as the skunk could not see how ferocious I was, we did OK.

Skunkmobile

I hand-carried the gift-wrapped skunk to the front yard, where I attached the cage to the top of my Jeep Cherokee. The skunk remained a real gentleman or perhaps lady.   I had no desire to check out the specifics.

A Secure Undisclosed Location

The skunk was transported to a Secure Undisclosed Location. We rode over some very bumpy roads, which was pressing our luck. Again, he withheld his fire. Could it be the intelligence information about the skunks WMD capability was faulty?

The Release

Using the ten-foot pole, I unwrapped the live trap. I expected the insurgent to make a run for the hills once I opened the door to the trap. Instead, he looked out, saw me, and returned to the cage. It took about ten minutes of coaxing to get him to leave.

Mission Accomplished

The insurgent finally took off—straight for my wife who was waiting in the get-away car. A little more coaxing sent him off toward the woods—Mission Accomplished.

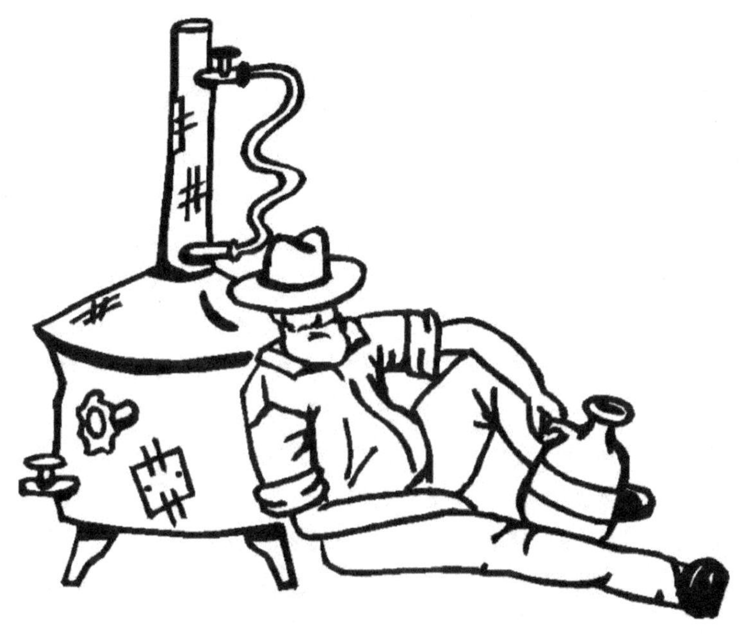

*M.A.C.H.O. Night

Spring does not come early in Michigan's Upper Peninsula, and the spring of '23 was no exception. The first of May found the snow in the woods still a foot deep, and large drifts were abundant in open fields. Yoopers, as the natives of the U.P. refer to themselves, were just emerging from their quasi-hibernation and beginning to stir. It had been a long, hard winter, and snowshoes had been the only reliable means of transportation. Still, the Yoopers were a happy lot—they didn't know any better. They were unaware that in lower Wisconsin, people were picking wild flowers, and snowdrifts were a distant memory. True Yoopers never left the U.P. Having been told by other Yoopers this was God's country, they felt no desire to wander.

No one ever came to the U.P. in the wintertime. At Bear Creek, no one came to town in the summer time. They might pass through the town or be forced to spend a night in the hotel above the Snake Pit Saloon, but no one came to Bear Creek. There was no reason to come to Bear Creek, as nothing ever happened at Bear Creek. But the Yoopers who lived there didn't care—they didn't know any better.

Bear Creek, located above the Wisconsin border in Michigan's Upper Peninsula, does offer the usual amenities. It has the Bear Creek Cafe and the Snake Pit Saloon, now allegedly dry with prohibition. There is also the Bear Creek Gazette and the Bear Creek Hardware and Feed store. For those unfortunate travelers stranded in Bear Creek, there is lodging available at a reasonable price above the Snake Pit Saloon. It may not be quiet or clean, but it is the only hotel in town.

The mayor of Bear Creek was one P.C. Taylor, who was also owner and manager of the Bear Creek Cafe. No one seemed to know what the P.C. stood for, and P.C. wasn't volunteering any information. He had lost his right eye in his youth while working as a logger and now wore a black patch over the eye. P.C. was elected mayor as a joke, having been nominated by Silas Kronschnabell during a drunken brawl. The job had no salary since the town had no taxes or other means of income. P.C. took the job seriously and strutted around town in his three-piece suit, frequently looking at his pocket watch, which always registered quarter past one. Occasionally he would cut a ribbon at an opening of a new store; but for the most part, he spent his time with his best friend Chief Red Weasel. Since the retirement of Chief Thunder Head, Weasel was the senior Indian Chief in the area, and the two heads of state had many a summit meeting down at their favorite fishing hole.

P.C.'s wife, Maggie, managed the cafe quite nicely without his help, and that was fine with her. She did have their seventeen-year-old daughter Jennifer to assist with some of the chores. Some say Maggie had been a real firebrand in her youth before she got religion. Now she was president of the Ladies Aid Society at the Bear Creek Methodist Church, and her old zeal was directed against liquor and wild women, both of which could be obtained in ample quantities at the Snake Pit Saloon—despite prohibition.

An early May thaw had melted most of the snow but the morning remained cool even by Yooper standards, forcing the Bear Creek Economics Club to pay homage to the potbelly stove in the front of the Mel Barker's Hardware and Feed Store. Located in the center of the store, the potbelly stove, now glowing hot, made the room more hospitable, one of the reasons members of the Bear Creek Economics

Club gathered at the Hardware and Feed Store each morning. Mel couldn't remember the last time they discussed the local economy, but the name gave the group respectability and purpose, unlike the Methodist Church's Ladies Aid Society, which everyone knew only met for gossip sessions.

Silas Kronschnabell, proprietor of the Bear Creek Gazette, called the Bear Creek Economics Club to order. Frenchie, a young French Canadian, was in the process of beating P.C. Taylor at checkers despite P.C.'s ill-conceived efforts to cheat. A small wager made the game worthwhile. Both players felt cheating was a finely honed skill, adding a new and stimulating dimension to the game. The outcome depended as much on cheating skills as expertise in the fundamentals of the game. The fact that Frenchie had recently married P.C.'s daughter and was now P.C.'s son-in-law only added to the competition. Except for Frenchie, the club members were in their fifties.

Aside from the checker game, little was happening at the routine meeting of the Bear Creek Economics Club, and members were sitting around in abject boredom.

"What this town needs is some good, old-fashioned excitement," Mel said after spending ten minutes watching a spider spinning a web over a pitchfork that was hanging on the wall. "We never have a bank robbery or have a citizen abducted by aliens."

"Don't have a bank in town," Silas reminded Mel, "and no self-respecting alien would be caught dead in Bear Creek. Even they think Bear Creek is too dull." An alien abduction did have possibilities, Silas decided. As editor of the Bear Creek Gazette, Silas was always on the lookout for quality news.

"I'm willing to help build a bank and throw in a couple of bucks if you can find someone with the energy to rob it." Mel wondered if spiders ever got bored spinning webs.

"How about a M.A.C.H.O. night?" Silas suggested.

"What's a M.A.C.H.O. night?" Frenchie asked.

"It stands for Men Advocating a Completely Hedonic Outing," Silas replied. "It's a night dedicated to male bonding, where we shed the shackles of domestic servitude and rise up as free men, free of the banal bondage of boring bleakness, free of the malignant microcosms of the maladroit mainstream, free of the..."

"Basically we sit around, play cards, and have a nip or two of P.C.'s corn liquor," Mel said, cutting short Silas's soliloquy. Since prohibition, the only available liquid entertainment came from P.C.'s still, which by necessity was hidden in the deep woods, far from the prying eyes of their self-righteous wives.

"I suppose we could meet at the still," P.C. suggested. "There's a good place for a bonfire, and with a few lanterns in the trees, we'd have plenty of light for playing poker."

"Are you talking about spending the entire night?" Frenchie asked.

"Unless the liquor runs out," Mel replied.

"I'd have to check with Jennifer first."

The members of the Bear Creek Economics Club looked at each other. This boy needs help, they decided. Silas walked over to Frenchie and placed his arm around Frenchie's shoulder.

"Look at it this way," Silas suggested. "Jennifer loves you, doesn't she?"

"Yes, I guess she does."

"If she really loves you, she'd want you to have a good time, wouldn't she?"

"I suppose so."

"Even though Jennifer would prefer that you come with us, she would be under great pressure from the rest of the women, misguided as they may be. Women are good people, mind you, but they're obsessed with this perverted sense of morality that stymies their imagination and creativity, limiting the wholesome appreciation of life. Without men they would have absolutely no fun at all, which is why they marry us. These malignant moral values are forced upon unsuspecting girls in their formative years when they're still young and impressionable. That peer pressure can be unbearable. We know; we're married to them. You'll actually be doing Jennifer a favor by not telling her. You really do love her, don't you?" Silas took out his pipe and filled it with tobacco.

"Of course I do."

"If you really love her, it's your duty not to tell her and avoid placing her in an awkward position." Silas lit the pipe and took a drag, producing a cloud of blue smoke.

"I have to tell her something. Can't just not come home."

"You and I are going to Marquette to check on the market for potatoes," P.C. suggested. "That'll cover both of us."

"I have to go to Escanaba to see about parts for my printing press," Silas decided.

"I may have to be out of town at a hardware convention in Green Bay," Mel added.

"Are ya sure this'll be all right?" Frenchie asked.

"If you really love your wife, it's the only option," Silas said. "We do it all the time, and we love our wives."

"I guess you guys have more experience in this area than I do."

"Then it's settled. We'll meet at the still next Friday," Silas said. "It might be wise to arrive at different times. We don't want to draw undue attention."

***

"Good morning, girls," Maggie said as she opened the May meeting of the Bear Creek Methodist Church's Ladies Aid Society. "I'm now going to turn the program over to Trudy who has a neat idea for a church fund-raiser."

"The other day I was thinking of ways we could raise money for a coal furnace." Trudy stood up to speak, feeling it added more authority to her statements. "As you all know we only have a wood burning stove to heat the church, and that doesn't heat the basement at all. It makes it very cold for the children in Sunday school. I'm, therefore, suggesting we have a potato sausage sale."

"Potato sausage? What's that?" Agnes asked.

"It's made of chopped onions and potatoes mixed in with ground beef and pork. Add some salt and pepper, stuff it into some animal casings, and presto, you have potato sausage."

"How do you expect to make any money with the potato sausage, sell it to ourselves?" Agnes wasn't totally convinced.

"No, of course not. That would be silly. What good would it do to make potato sausage and then sell it to ourselves? We sell it to our husbands."

"Maybe they won't buy the sausage."

"They will if we tell them to."

"But our husbands won't know how to cook the potato sausage after they buy it," Mrs. Olson pointed out.

"We'll have to cook the sausage, but by then we'll have their money."

It all made sense when Trudy explained it that way.

"We have a sausage stuffer at the cafe that will fill the casings with sausage," Maggie informed the ladies.

"I think it's a great idea," Mrs. Olson decided.

"All in favor?" Maggie asked.

"Aye."

"OK by me."

"Let's do it."

"I'm for it."

"Motion carried."

"When is a good time?" Agnes asked.

"Friday would be a good time for Jennifer and me," Maggie said. "Pa and Frenchie will be in Marquette checking on the potato market for next summer. Might as well do it when they're not around."

"Friday is good for me also. Mel has to go to a hardware convention in Green Bay."

"Silas will be in Escanaba checking on parts for his printing press."

"That's convenient. All of our husbands will be gone at the same time," Trudy noted.

"That's too convenient," Maggie said.

"What about you, Mrs. Olson?"

"My husband will also be out of town."

"I smell a rat," Maggie said, summing up the feelings of all present.

"What do you think they're up to?"

"Probably a night of gambling and hard liquor."

"They're not meeting anywhere in town."

"I have a feeling if we find where they're meeting, we'll find their still."

"I think you're all wrong," Jennifer said. "Frenchie would never lie to me. If he says he's going to Marquette to check on the potato market, then he's going to Marquette to check on the potato market."

The members of the Bear Creek Methodist Church's Ladies Aid Society looked at each other. This girl needs help, they decided. Agnes walked over to Jennifer and placed her arm around Jennifer's shoulder.

"Look at it this way," Agnes suggested. "Frenchie loves you, doesn't he?"

"Yes, of course he does."

"If he really loves you, he'll expect you to use your best judgment to care for his needs. Men cry out for guidance and stability. They do best in a structured environment. That's why they marry us."

That's not why Frenchie married me, Jennifer thought. He had other things on his mind—and he didn't need any guidance either.

"They don't have the internal strength to fight off temptation like we do," Agnes continued. "It's up to us to provide that moral guidance they so desperately crave. It's not that men are bad, they just don't know any better."

"Well, I guess you women have been married longer than I have." Jennifer wasn't convinced, but didn't feel up to further argument.

"The bottom line is men are children that never grew up. Their hearts may be in the right place, but they can't be trusted." The rest of the women nodded in agreement.

"Where do we go from here?" Maggie asked, returning to the problem at hand.

"I say we follow them and see if they lead us to their still," Trudy suggested. "Then we smash the still and take no prisoners!"

"It would be best if only a small group tailed them," Agnes said. "Maybe Trudy and I could tail them and come back for the rest of you after we find their still."

"Everyone in favor of Agnes's motion?" Maggie asked.

The motion passed unanimously.

***

It had long been rumored that the elusive still was located east of town. Based on this information, Agnes and Trudy posted their lookout on a rocky outcrop overlooking the only road leading east. From their lofty perch, they could observe any travelers who might ply the road below. If they were wrong and the still wasn't east of town, they would know within the next half-hour. Mel was scheduled to leave the hardware store for his meeting in Green Bay forthwith.

They weren't disappointed. A dark shadow could be seen slinking along the edge of the road. From their distant viewpoint, it was impossible to identify the scoundrel, but he was obviously up to no good. Like a common criminal, he frequently looked over his shoulder to ensure he wasn't being followed.

"There he is." Agnes said, pointing to the figure walking on the road.

"Let me take a look through Mel's telescope." Trudy lifted a telescope to her right eye. According to

Mel, the telescope was given to him by Teddy Roosevelt himself. The story became more embellished with each telling.

"It's Mel all right. I would recognize that scraggly beard anywhere," Trudy said. "Watch him and see where he goes,"

Mel continued east for three-quarters of a mile before turning north into the woods. A tall white pine marked the point of his departure from the road.

It took ten minutes for Agnes and Trudy to descend from their rocky lookout to the road below. By the time they arrived, Mel was gone. A trail did lead into the woods, splitting frequently into a maze of sub trails.

"What do we do now?" Agnes asked. "He could've taken any of these trails."

"We wait," Trudy replied. "There'll be others."

"At least we know the conclave is east of town."

"We need to hide," Trudy said. "When the next lying varmint comes along, we'll follow him until he leads us to the others."

"It won't be easy following him without being seen."

"Not to worry. I haven't been listening to Mel's war stories for nothing."

Trudy, finding a small mud puddle left over from a recent rain, scooped up some of the dark mud and carefully smeared the gooey mess over her face and hands until her skin was totally darkened.

"Ugh, surely you don't expect me to cover my body with that filthy dirt?" Agnes asked, as she watched in disgust. "There is no telling what kinds of bugs and creepy organisms are crawling in that mud."

"The girls are depending on us," Trudy said, smearing mud on Agnes's face.

"They're still going to be able to see us.

"That's because we're not done yet." Trudy cut some branches from a small bush, sticking them in her shirt, under her belt, and any other place that would secure the branches. A few vines were added to the ensemble to give a little variety. Agnes did likewise, and the two ladies disappeared into the foliage.

"The key is to freeze and not move if someone is looking at you," one bush said to the other bush.

The two camouflaged commandos didn't have to vegetate long before the next fugitive from female fetters arrived on the scene.

"That has to be Silas," said Bush Number One.

"Don't move. Let him walk past us," commanded Bush Number Two. "OK, let's follow him," Bush Number Two whispered when Silas passed the brush pile.

The brush pile watched as Silas continued down the path, turning right at a fork in the trail.

"Freeze!" Bush Number One whispered, and Bush Number Two immediately froze. Silas had turned around and was staring at the brush pile. Seeing nothing out of place, he returned to his brisk stroll.

***

Silas made no attempt to conceal that he was renting a horse from Ollie Olson's livery stable. After saddling up, he headed back into the center of town instead of heading directly toward Escanaba. He was careful to stop and say hello to any friends along the way, especially women folk, letting them know that, indeed, he was on his way to Escanaba. After much fanfare, he rode off to the west only to circle around behind the livery stable where he returned the horse with a wink to Ollie. Where he was going, he wouldn't need a horse.

Silas gave the town a wide berth as he circled around to the road leading east. He continued down the road until he came to a branch lying on the road. It was nothing more than a twig that had recently been broken free from its attachment. Most folks would have ignored it, but Silas turned down a trail suggested by the broken end of the twig. He came to a fork in the trail, and another broken twig pointed toward the correct path.

This is easy, Silas thought. Agnes didn't suspect a thing. It's amazing how naive women can be. It just proves the natural superiority of men over women. That's why women should never have been given the right to vote. The female mind doesn't have the capability of complex thought, which is why they're always outwitted by men.

Silas thought he heard some noise behind him and turned to look. He would have sworn that bush had moved. It must have been the wind, but none of the other bushes were moving, and he didn't feel a breeze. Maybe it was a small bird moving among the branches. Either way, it was none of his concern, and he turned back to the trail.

It was a three-mile walk to the still, and by the time Silas arrived, it was already starting to get dark. Mel, P.C., and several other men had arrived earlier and had set up a table consisting of wooden planks across sawhorses. The trunk of a white pine had been cut into sections, which were being used as stools. Let the drinking and card playing begin.

Should be enough corn liquor to keep them going deep into the night, Silas decided after surveying the operation. There were several vats of finished product waiting to be sampled while other vats, containing fermenting corn syrup, awaited their turn at the still. A fire under a copper kettle confirmed that the still was in full operation. The flickering light from the fire cast shadows that danced on the bushes at the edge of the clearing. If one didn't know better, one would swear the bushes were moving. Silas filled his mug with corn whiskey and headed for the table. "Deal me in," he informed the others.

***

"We were right," Agnes told the hastily assembled group of women. "They're partying at their still."

"There were several vats of finished whiskey as well as two vats of corn syrup waiting to be distilled." Trudy scratched at her neck. She wished they had been more selective in choosing the leaves and vines to stuff into their shirts. She was hoping the itching was from the mud remaining on their faces and necks, but she feared the worst. She had a strong allergy to poison ivy.

"The trail is marked by fresh cut branches with the cut end pointing in the correct direction," Agnes informed the crew. "It's on the other side of Moose Lake."

"I suggest we meet back here in thirty minutes with flashlights and axes," Maggie suggested. "First we destroy the still, and then everyone is in charge of collaring her own husband."

***

By midnight, a good portion of the male citizens of Bear Creek had arrived at the party, requiring the addition of several new poker tables. Greenbacks were passed freely back and forth as the participants, now well lubricated with the one hundred proof corn whisky, bet on trivial hands.

The fire under the copper kettle provided warmth for those with an occasional chill, but failed to provide adequate light for serious poker players. Therefore, kerosene lanterns hung from the trees along the periphery of the card tables. Neither the light from the fire nor the light from the lanterns penetrated into the depths of the surrounding woods, providing safe haven for any stalking predators. A wary observer, however, would have noted the occasional flicker of a flashlight. A wary observer would have noted the unexplained snapping of a twig. A wary observer would have heard the low whispers protruding from the darkness. But there were no wary observers to provide advance warning. There were no wary observers to sound the alarm before the predators pounced upon their prey. The predators slowly but methodically closed in upon their quarry. There would be no escape. They would give no quarter.

A soprano voice yelled, "Attack!" and a dozen Amazons wielding axes, hatchets, and sledgehammers descended upon the panic stricken men. The still and wooden vats of fermented produce were the first to go, as axes changed the vats into kindling wood and the copper still into scrap metal.

"It's an ambush, run for your lives!" one of the more sober men yelled out. "It's every man for himself!" Men scattered in every direction.

Many people would find it difficult to navigate through the woods in the daylight even when sober. It can be more difficult at night when the finely honed skills of the northern woodsman are mitigated by the influence of one hundred-proof corn whisky. Needless to say, clunking noises could be heard as hard heads ran into harder trees. Other fugitives howled as they became entwined in briar patches, and moans could be heard coming from every corner of the periphery. The predators, with flashlights in hand, followed the moans until every generic husband had been subdued by the ear and returned to center stage for prisoner exchange. Once all of the women were reunited with their inebriated spouses, the long trek home began. Penance would begin in the morning.

***

Silas tossed a peeled potato into the stainless steel pot filled with water. The members of the Bear Creek Economics Club who surrounded the pot cringed in pain as the noise of the splash echoed throughout the church basement. From the quality of his headache, Silas assumed he must have had a good time the night before. He reached into the bag beside him to retrieve a fresh potato. There were many more to peel.

"I don't know why we have to peel all of these potatoes," Frenchie said.

"That's the way life is," P.C. informed his son-in-law.

"Have you seen how they make the sausage?" Frenchie asked. "They grind up pork and beef and mix in potatoes and onions. Then they stuff it into cow guts. What idiot is going to buy that stuff?"

"We're the idiots who'll buy it," Mel said.

"Well, I'm not going to buy any of it," Frenchie informed the group.

"How's the potato peeling coming?" Jennifer asked from the door to the church kitchen where the women were busy stuffing the sausage. "We need more potatoes. We're expecting to sell a lot of sausage. We're doing so well, we've decided to make this an annual event. Frenchie, be a dear and buy five pounds of sausage, O.K.?" Jennifer returned to the kitchen without waiting for an answer.

"Five pounds? I suspect the fine for the rest of us will be closer to fifteen pounds," Mel said.

"They're letting him off easy because it's his first offense," Silas decided.

"How come we are doing all this?" Frenchie asked.

"It beats three weeks on the couch. You do the vice, you pay the price. If you get caught on a M.A.C.H.O. night, you got to pay the dues."

"How often do you have M.A.C.H.O. nights?"

"Once or twice a year."

"Do you always get caught?"

"Shucks no!" Mel said indignantly. "Why just four years ago—or was it five years ago?"

"I think it was five years ago," Silas said. "It was just after the end of the Great War."

"Anyway," Mel continued, "P.C. and Red Weasel made this fishing raft out of four army surplus inflatable boats by building a wooden platform over them. It was so big you could've danced on it."

"Mighty fine raft at that," P.C. said.

"We hung lanterns from corner posts and built a canvas canopy in case it rained. We added a few tables for cards, and bingo, we had a perfect M.A.C.H.O. platform."

"The women didn't find out?" Frenchie asked.

"Oh, they found out all right," Mel said, "but they couldn't do anything about it. We were a quarter mile off shore."

"We must have partied until three in the morning."

"Yeah, that's when P.C. added more kerosene to the lanterns."

"The kerosene wouldn't have caught fire if it hadn't been for that stogie Mel was chewing on," P.C. pointed out in his defense.

"Then what happened?" Frenchie asked.

"Well, inflatable rafts don't do well around fire," Silas said, "and the wooden platform didn't do much better."

"Did they ever find Hank Heikkinen's body?" Mel asked.

"Someone thought they saw him in Montreal. Maybe he's still alive and hiding from his wife."

"At least he doesn't have to peel these stupid potatoes," Mel said, tossing another peeled potato into the pot of water.

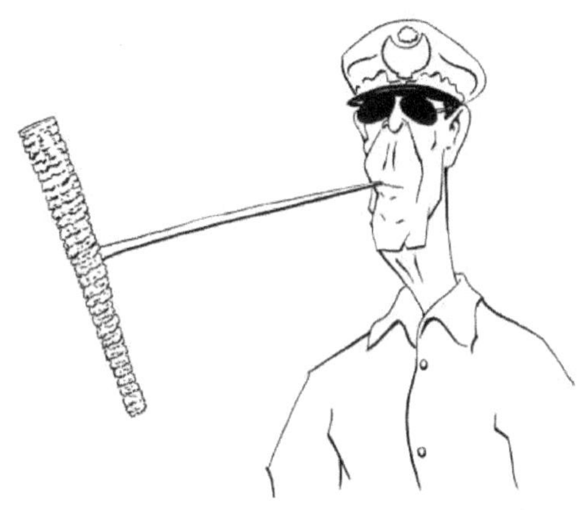

*The Yooper War

The 82nd Airborne Division was marching off to war. A reliable informant had suggested Finland had Weapons of Mass Destruction and wanted to turn the U.P. into a Finnish colony. The president was left with no choice but to declare war on the U.S. and invade the U.P. Several dozen transport planes waited along the edge of the runway while paratroopers, weighted down with eighty pounds of combat gear, filed aboard. This was the day they had trained for.

This was the day they would make history. This was the day they would make an airborne assault to defend American soil. Their objective: seize the strategic town of Bear Creek.

Actually, it was night, illuminated only by a quarter moon, which invited mishap, but Major General Amos "Mad Dog" Rottweiler, commander of the 82nd Airborne, was not one to worry. That's why he had subordinates. Let them worry. He rested his hands on his pearl-handled revolvers and watched his men embark upon the planes. A pair of mirrored sunglasses covered his eyes. He felt generals looked cool with mirrored sunglasses. It made night vision difficult, but that was the price you paid for being cool.

"General, the men are all aboard and ready to go."

Mad Dog Rottweiler recognized the voice of his Command Sergeant Major. It was coming from his left. He could make out the camo-painted face of the Sergeant Major over the rim of his glasses. "Guess it's time for us to climb aboard." This would be a good day. Maybe he would get that third star. General Rottweiler extracted his corncob pipe from his shirt pocket and filled it with tobacco.

Mad Dog was a fightin' general. He would jump with his troops. He only regretted it had to be at night. There would be no photographer to immortalize the moment he stepped aboard the plane. No newsreel of the commanding general, with camo-painted face, leading his troops into harm's way. It would have looked good on the six o'clock news. He was about to ignite his bowl of pipe tobacco, but decided against it. He wasn't particularly fond of the pipe, and without the presence of TV cameras, the corncob pipe served no useful purpose. He would save it for later.

General Rottweiler followed the Sergeant Major to a waiting plane. His plane filled with headquarters staff and radiomen would lead the formation. The planes were under the control of the air force, and airmen with red flashlights began guiding planes toward the runway. If they were to fly in formation, it was imperative the planes get airborne as quickly as possible. Air traffic controllers diverted all commercial traffic from the U.P. This night sky belonged to the 82nd Airborne.

The General sat on the bench next to Col. Hansen, one of his staff officers. Paratroopers with painted faces, tight fitting helmets, and camouflaged fatigues lined both sides of the aircraft. In the red light they all looked the same.

The plane was soon airborne and flying a holding pattern while they waited for other planes to join the formation. A few minutes later the entire formation turned toward the Upper Peninsula. The pilots turned on their running lights to reduce the chances of mid-air collisions. They weren't worried about airborne attacks. Harriers from the Iwo Jima would join them shortly, providing fighter escort to the insertion point. Finland had an air force, but even if they flew over the pole, the U.P. stretched beyond their range. The Yoopers were on their own.

General Rottweiler removed his sunglasses and looked out his window. Dozens of red lights, each representing a plane, blinked in the darkness. It was an impressive formation, probably the largest nighttime airborne assault since WW II. The name Rottweiler would be itched into the history books tonight.

"TWENTY MINUTES TO THE DROP ZONE," the plane's jumpmaster yelled at the paratroopers. The paratroopers sat quietly as if they hadn't heard. Each paratrooper had his own private thoughts and his own self-doubts. At the end of the row a young man crossed himself. It never hurt to seek the blessing of the Sky Pilot.

The bureaucrats in Washington selected the Seney Stretch, a boring twenty-five mile section of real estate between Seney on the east and Shingleton on the west, as the drop zone. The two bordering towns were connected by a section of M-28 that could have been drawn on the map with a straight edge.

The maps in Washington revealed a perfectly flat stretch of land, perfect for an airborne assault. The fact that it was in the center of the U.P. and not far from Bear Creek was another asset. The paratroopers would reassemble upon landing and make a quick march on the town. The rapid conquest of Bear Creek—part of the shock and awe—would demoralize any resistance.

What the maps in Washington didn't show were the cedar swamps, peat bogs and jack pine, perfect for deer hunters but useless for any civilized endeavor. The only significant establishment was the Seney Wildlife Refuge where the Federal Government spent endless tax dollars encouraging geese, ducks, and sandhill cranes to make use of the swamps, as if they really needed encouragement.

"FIVE MINUTES TO THE DROP ZONE." The jumpmaster seemed unusually cheerful. He didn't have to jump.

Upon command, the paratroopers stood up and attached their static lines to the overhead cable. Each man checked the man in front of him to ensure all items were buttoned down and secured. Since this was a combat jump, there were no reserve chutes. Each man had one chance.

General Rottweiler felt a blast of air as the jumpmaster opened the door on the side of the plane. Mad Dog casually strolled to the front of the line, aware that all eyes were on him—as they should be. He clipped his static line to the overhead cable in front of the others. He was a fightin' general, and he would jump first.

"ONE MINUTE TO GO." The jumpmaster watched a red light controlled by the pilot. Timing was everything. Jumping one or two minutes early or late could place the paratroopers miles from their target.

The red light turned green, and the jumpmaster yelled, "GO." But the General was already halfway out the door. The other paratroopers followed the General like lemmings leaping off a cliff into the darkness—the Yooper War had begun.

***

Major General Amos "Mad Dog" Rottweiler adjusted his mirrored sunglasses. A general needed to be cool despite the hardships of combat. The coolness was offset by the torn shirt and trousers. The left sleeve of his shirt was missing, and scratches covered his arm. They were the result of Mad Dog's unfortunate encounter with a belligerent spruce tree on his descent. Just for spite, he would have the tree cut down once he assembled his troops. You don't do that to Mad Dog Rottweiler and get away with it.

The Command Sergeant Major missed the trees but discovered one of the Seney Stretch's many swamps and was now huddling around a makeshift campfire trying to thaw out. The Upper Peninsula mornings can be cool for those wearing wet clothing. He was roasting a pair of soggy socks on a tag elder branch. A steady flow of white steam confirmed the effectiveness of the operation.

The only other surviving member of the headquarters group was the radioman who was diligently monitoring reports from various segments of the 82nd Airborne. He had managed to avoid both trees and swamps.

General Rottweiler spread a map on the ground. According to his GPS, he should be about here. He placed an "X" on the spot. They were not far from Bear Creek. He would assemble his troops and immediately march on the town. The town would be his by evening. "Have you contacted all the units?" Rottweiler asked with the impatience of a general.

"I reached a few, sir, but it's mostly garbled." The radioman fiddled with his dials. "It appears the wind scattered men all over God's creation. Most of them are beyond the range of our radio."

That was not what Mad Dog wanted to hear. He considered shooting the messenger but decided against it. He currently had two people in his command, and he would need both of them. "What about the ones you did contact? Are they regrouping?"

"That appears to be a problem too. They can't distinguish members of the 82nd from the native Yoopers. They don't know who's who."

The General reconsidered shooting the messenger. "How hard can that be? Members of the 82nd are dressed in camouflaged fatigues and have their faces covered with green paint."

"That's the problem, sir. This is bow-hunting season. Everybody is wearing camouflaged fatigues and paint on their faces. Yoopers are hanging from tree stands and hiding behind every bush. I think they have us out numbered."

The General swatted at a mosquito molesting his exposed arm. "Damn Yoopers!" This was only a minor setback, but Mad Dog did not like setbacks. "Keep on the radio, son. I want to know every change in our status before it changes... What's that horrid smell?" The General looked over at his Sergeant

Major—the white steam from the socks had changed to black smoke.

***

Beagle one, this is sawbones eight three, come in." PFC Stan Richards listened for a reply but was not surprised when no reply was forthcoming from his radio. He had been trying most of the night without results. The wind must have blown him too far from battalion headquarters.

He hadn't seen anyone from his unit since he jumped. He had a compass, but without a map, he could be walking away from his unit. With land this flat, he wasn't sure a map would be of value. The best he could do was wander around and periodically try the radio. With a bit of luck, he might make contact. "Beagle one, this is sawbones eight three, come in."

As a medic with company A, he didn't normally carry a radio. The company commander gave him the honor in retaliation for declaring his regular radioman unfit for duty because of a broken leg. The commander remained convinced the radioman was malingering despite X-rays confirming the fracture.

Richards looked around, trying to decide which direction to go. For all he knew, he could be walking in circles. The land was flat and what few depressions did exist, Mother Nature converted to swamps. Jack pine and the occasional white pine covered the rest of the land. Thorny bushes filled any gaps in the coverage.

Richards took the path of least resistance and headed for a tall white pine. "This is sawbones eight three, is anyone out there?" As usual, there was no response. He was beginning to wonder if his batteries were dead. It wouldn't be the first time the military had screwed up.

Richards removed his pack and radio at the base of the white pine and sat down to do some serious thinking. Wandering around the woods was getting him nowhere. At least the ground here was dry, and he had the white pine as a backrest. Eventually, he would need food and water, but for now he had a full canteen and two MRE's in the cargo pockets of his pants. He opened one of the MRE's and extracted a candy bar. He could think better while eating.

With nothing better to do, he keyed the mike on the radio. "Just in case anyone is listening, this is sawbones eight three." Richards set the mike on the ground to enjoy his candy bar.

"It's nice to hear another voice."

Did he hear right? Richards grabbed the mike. "This is PFC Richards from Company A. Which company are you with?"

"Company C."

"Anyone else with you?" Richards asked.

"Nope, just me. You wouldn't have an extra candy bar, would you? That one looks pretty good."

How did he know about the candy bar, Richards wondered. "Where are you?"

"Up here."

Richards look up into the tree. A fellow paratrooper dangled from his camouflaged parachute twelve feet above the ground. With his painted face and camouflaged fatigues, he blended in with the tree.

"What ya doing up there?"

"The buckle on my harness is jammed, and I dropped my bayonet, so I can't cut myself loose. Been sort of hanging around most of the night."

"You're lucky. It's dry up there. I spent the night wandering through swamps."

"My name's Corporal Higgins, John Higgins."

"Stan Richards."

"About that candy bar, my MRE's are in my backpack. I can't get to them."

"Right, sure." Richards tossed a candy bar up to Corporal Higgins.

"Thank you… I was getting hungry."

"I suppose your predicament has its drawbacks," Richards said after a moment of thought.

"You don't know the worst of it. I can pee from up here, but that's about it."

"You will let me know?"

"Let you know?"

"I mean…if you have to pee…being down below and everything."

"Sure, that would only be common courtesy."

With no better plan of action, Richards sat at the base of the tree to discuss women, sports, women, politics, and women. He found Corporal Higgins quite knowledgeable about sports and politics, but he didn't understand women either.

"I think someone's coming," Corporal Higgins said from his superior location. Moments later two men in camouflaged uniforms and green painted faces stepped into the clearing. Each one carried a compound bow and had a quiver of arrows strapped to his back.

"Ya see dat twelve point buck, eh?" one of them asked Richards.

"Looky, Toivo. Dare's another one up in dat tree," the second one said. "Yoose guys have goot tree stand."

Richard stood up. "My name's PFC Stan Richards…and this is Corporal John Higgins." Richards pointed to the man in the tree.

"Da name's Eino Luokkala and dis is my no goot brodder-in-law Toivo."

"What unit you with?" Richards asked.

"Unit? We's from Camp Destitute."

"We…Corporal Higgins and I…got separated from our units. We were wondering if we could go back to Camp Destitute with you?"

"Ya, we play poker and drink beer."

"The problem is that my friend, here," Richards gestured toward Higgins. "He can't get down from the tree."

"My no goot brodder-in-law, Toivo, can fix dat."

Without further discussion Toivo took an arrow from his quiver. The blades of the broadhead were constructed of high-carbon steel and honed to a razor's edge. A single shot severed the strap above Higgins's left shoulder, sending him swinging back and forth from the strap above his right shoulder. A second arrow also found its mark, and Higgins plummeted to the ground.

Corporal Higgins hit hard, leading Richards to wonder if Higgins would be his first casualty. Grabbing his aid bag, Richards ran over to the crumpled paratrooper, but Higgins had fallen on a soft carpet of pine needles. Other than being shaken up, he seemed to be no worse for the wear.

"Yoose guys follow us." Eino headed down a path.

"I hope someone has a fire going back at your camp." Richards felt his boots slosh with each step. "I've been wading through swamps all night. Got a bit of a chill."

"We put yoose guys in sauna. Dat'll warm yoose up."

Richards and Higgins fell back slightly, and Richards whispered into Higgins's ear. "Where do you think these guys came from? There're not from A company."

"I think there're from a special unit…like snipers. Did you see how they shoot those bows? Probably a special commando unit."

"They sure talk funny."

"Maybe so, but if we follow them back to their base camp, we may find someone who knows where our units are."

***

General Amos "Mad Dog" Rottweiler used the last of the Scotch tape. His fatigues had ripped during his encounter with the tree, and the tears were increasing in size. Hopefully, the Sergeant Major's Scotch tape would prevent further destruction. Even with mirrored sunglasses, it is hard to look cool in a torn uniform. There was nothing he could do about the missing right sleeve, but he would proudly wear the rest of his uniform, tattered that it might be.

"General, sir?"

"Yes, Sergeant Major, what is it?"

"Sir, I'm afraid we have bad news... We made radio contact with some of our men."

"That's bad news? That's what we've been waiting for. Now we can assemble our men and march on Bear Creek."

"Sir, the radioman said the contact was with PFC Richards and Corporal Higgins. They have been taken prisoner by the enemy but were able to radio in a brief report."

"And what was the nature of this report?"

"It...It isn't pretty, sir," the Sergeant Major said with a quiver in his voice.

"Pull yourself together, Sergeant Major. We're U.S. Soldiers!"

"Sir, they were tortured!"

"Tortured?"

"They stripped them naked and locked them in a cedar box. Then they pumped it full of steam until our men could hardly breathe. After they became totally dehydrated, they were taken out and drenched in ice water. The Yoopers laughed at them and apologized for not having a snow bank to throw them into!"

"The savages!"

"That's not all, sir. After they threw ice water on them, the Yoopers beat their backs with birch boughs."

"Mark my words, Sergeant Major; they'll pay for this. I'm bringing them up on war crimes when this is over. No one treats Mad Dog Rottweiler's men like that and gets away with it... Any word from other units?"

"The radioman says he's getting garbled messages but nothing he can understand. He thinks the other units were scattered too far apart by the wind."

"Well, gather up what men we have. We're marching on Bear Creek. We can't wait for the entire division to arrive."

"But sir, with the radioman and me, we only have two enlisted men. How are we going to take Bear Creek?"

"Leadership, my boy. You two are being led by General Amos 'Mad Dog' Rottweiler!"

***

Light from the campfire danced across the General's reflective sunglasses as he sat motionless in front of the fire. If the General hadn't been roasting a venison steak, the Sergeant Major would have assumed he was asleep.

The Sergeant Major removed his boots and messaged his feet. He had a generous crop of friction blisters sprouting up under his damp socks. He hoped his socks would dry if he held his feet near the fire. The aroma from the venison steak at the end of his roasting stick momentarily diverted his attention. He had forgotten what a forced march could do to one's appetite. His mouth began to water. Venison was better fare than the MRE's they were issued.

"Sergeant Major, I been thinking." The General proclaimed his steak done and took a bite. "We should give the citizens of Bear Creek an opportunity to surrender. Much as I'd like a good fight, it's the only humane thing to do."

"Sir, our deployment here in the Seney Stretch may not be progressing as smoothly as it would appear on first impression."

"Nonsense, Sergeant Major, it couldn't be better. Here we are sitting around a campfire eating fresh venison steaks like a couple of Boy Scouts; and if I read the map correctly, Bear Creek is only five miles away. We should be there in two, three hours tops. After we take the town, we can commandeer the local hotel for our headquarters and have a hot bath... By the way, where did we get the venison?"

"The radioman got it. He thought as long as everyone was deer hunting he would give it a try. He bagged a ten pointer."

"The meat's a little tough, but still better than MRE's," the General said. "Remind me to give the lad a commendation when this is over... Where is the boy? He's supposed to keep us in touch with the rest of the unit."

"He was arrested, sir."

"Arrested?"

"By the game warden. Apparently, in Michigan you aren't allowed to use grenades during bow season."

"What about the radio? That's our link to the other units." The General swatted at a mosquito lunching on his bare arm. The tape on his uniform had not survived the forced march through the dense undergrowth, and now both shirtsleeves were ripped off, much to the delight of numerous hungry mosquitoes.

"The game warden confiscated the radio too… That's what I mean, sir. There are only two of us left, and we have no communication with the rest of the battalion. We have nothing left to fight with. When General Wainwright was out of food and ammunition at Corregidor, he surrendered. There was no dishonor in it. They awarded him the Medal of Honor."

"Surrender? General Amos 'Mad Dog' Rottweiler never surrenders. Must I remind you we have both food and ammunition? As long as you have your M-16 and I have my trusty pearl-handled revolvers, we will fight to the finish!"

"It was just a thought, sir."

"I have no intention of spending the duration of the war locked naked in a cedar box—with or without steam. Get your boots on… We have five miles to go."

***

Major General Amos "Mad Dog" Rottweiler pushed aside some tag elders as he plowed his way through the brush. The tag elders snapped back like carriage whips, hitting the Sergeant Major who followed a few paces behind the General. The tag elders weren't as bad as the wild raspberries and a multitude of other thorny shrubs that reached out and tore at their clothing. The General's shirt, already torn from his encounter with the tree, had to be discarded as a total loss. The General took the loss particularly hard since it was the two stars on his shirt collar that proclaimed his rank. The pearled handled revolvers and the mirrored sunglasses should make his rank obvious to the astute observer, he rationalized.

"Sir?"

"Yes, Sergeant Major?"

"I hate to appear ungrateful for all the army has given me…three dehydrated meals a day…a sixty-hour workweek…a first-class sleeping bag, and an occasional cold shower; but don't you think the army sometimes asks too much from us?"

"And your point is, Sergeant Major?" The General swatted at a mosquito that was taking advantage of his bare chest. Some insects had no respect for rank.

"Well, sir, I been thinking we have done our best…under the circumstances." The Sergeant Major cleared his throat. "The army can't expect us to do the impossible."

"Are you suggesting we surrender again?"

"The army couldn't fault us for it, sir. We have nothing left to give. In a prison camp we could provide resistance... like they did in that old TV series."

"How much resistance can we provide from a steam-filled cedar box? Must I remind you we would also be naked! Definitely not appropriate attire for a general. The barbarians might even take away my mirrored sunglasses. No, we will never surrender. We will fight to the finish. We will fight to the last soldier. And in the end, we will be victorious."

"I hope you're right, sir. But I don't see how the two of us can overpower Bear Creek, even though it is a small town."

"That does make it difficult. I had planned on a larger force." The General mulled over the situation for a moment. "We'll have to stick to the basics. First we'll surround them."

"Surround them, sir?"

"Right. You'll come in from the north with your M-16 on full automatic. I'll come in from the south with both my pistols blazing. It's the classic technique of shock-and-awe."

The Sergeant Major was already beginning to feel the shock. "If you say so, sir."

"Let's pick up the pace. I want to secure Bear Creek before dark."

***

Silas Kronschnabell increased the torque on the flywheel's setscrew by an additional 12.4%. Just the same, he fortified his position before starting the press. The flywheel and flown off twice before. He didn't need any long-term disability. Silas pulled down on the power switch from his hiding spot behind a cart filled with rags. The press creaked, groaned, and then sputtered into a full roar. It sounded healthy. Silas peeked out from behind the rag cart but didn't see any flying parts, always a good sign. Paper from the large roll at the back of the machine was weaving through a series of rollers that fed it into the press. At the front of the press, freshly printed sports sections were stacking up. The Bear Creek Gazette was back in business. Silas programmed the press for five hundred copies.

It would take most of an hour to print the sports section, plenty of time to finish his weekly editorial. Silas gave the press another once over and retired to his office. Previously, he had considered writing an exposé on the Department of Natural Resource's decision to develop snowmobile trails through residential areas in flagrant disregard for the personal safety and wishes of local residents, a subject in which Silas had strong feelings. No one should have to endure convoys of noisy snowmobiles racing past their bedrooms at sixty miles per hour day and night. It was little wonder so many Yoopers wished to secede from Michigan.

He had also considered taking the federal government to task for closing K.I. Sawyer Air Force Base, pulling millions of defense dollars out of the local economy. Now, if he correctly understood the wire service reports, the Department of Defense was conducting military exercises in the U.P., but they weren't spending any money in the area. They were importing provisions from other states. The Upper Peninsula would receive no benefit from the exercise other than additional litter on the beaches.

Silas booted up his computer, still unsure which editorial to write. Eventually, he would write editorials on both subjects. Perhaps he should postpone the snowmobile issue until winter.

"Excuse me, Mr. Kronschnabell." Karla was standing in the doorway chewing gum. Her pink and red stripped hair hung at her shoulders.

"Don't you ever knock?" Sometimes he wondered why he kept her around. Being his wife's favorite niece was a point in her favor.

"Sorry, the door was open. It seemed silly to knock." Karla examined her green fingernails. She could have seriously damaged a nail knocking on the door.

"What can I do for you?"

"Got a guy out front who wants to talk to you. He's kind of weird."

"Weird?" He was surprised Karla would recognize weird.

"Yeah, he's wearing combat boots, yellow polka-dot boxer shorts, mirrored sunglasses, and nothing else… He's carrying a white flag."

"What's he want?"

"Something about a mad dog."

****

If you are a non-reader and finished reading these short stories, congratulations. You have done well. Perhaps it is time to remove those training wheels and put your new reading skills to a test run. I would suggest *Chogan and the Gray Wolf*. It was written for middle-grade boys, but the author now sells more books to adults for adults. The novel has half the word count as most adult novels, and the print is slightly larger (14 pt.). The stories follow the life of twelve-year-old Chogan who lives along the southern shore of Lake Superior one hundred years before Columbus. Chogan rescues an orphan wolf pup and raises it to adulthood. When he releases the wolf to the wild, the wolf returns to save Chogan's life.

Chogan and the Gray Wolf
Historically Accurate Native American Literature

It is 100 years B.C. (Before Columbus), and life is good for twelve-year-old Chogan and his ten-year-old sister until a Grizzly Bear terrorizes their Indian village along the southern shore of Lake Superior. The bear crushes wigwams with its massive weight and destroys precious strips of meat women had hung on racks to dry. Despite the danger, life must go on if Chogan and his family are to survive. Chogan and his sister venture into the forest of virgin white pine to check their snares and discover an orphaned wolf pup. The bear has killed the wolf pup's mother, and has left the pup to die.

Chogan adopts the young wolf knowing he must return the wolf to the wild at the end of the summer. Under Chogan's care, the wolf pup survives and grows to adulthood. The time comes when Chogan and the wolf must part and go their separate ways. The wolf quickly adapts to the wild but never forgets his friend. Chogan had saved the pup's life, and fate will soon provide the wolf with a chance to return the favor.

Amorous Spotted Slug for State Slug

Amorous Spotted Slug for State Slug

About the Author:

Larry Buege is a retired physician assistant who lives with his wife along the southern shore of Lake Superior. His literary work has won both regional and international awards. He writes in a variety of genres although his Chogan Native American Series is the most popular. The Native American Series follows an Ojibway family in the year 100 B.C. (Before Columbus). In addition to the short stories and novels, the author has been a frequent contributor to Primitive Technology magazine

Amorous Spotted Slug for State Slug